CARL HAFFNER'S

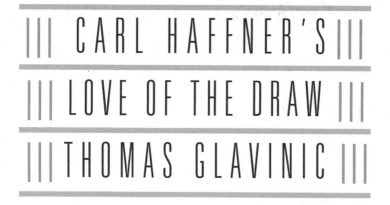

||| CARL HAFFNER'S |||
||| LOVE OF THE DRAW |||
||| THOMAS GLAVINIC |||

Translated from the German by
John Brownjohn

THE HARVILL PRESS
LONDON

First published with the title *Carl Haffners Liebe zum Unentschieden*
by Verlag Volk und Welt GmbH, Berlin, in 1998

First published in Great Britain in 1999
by The Harvill Press
2 Aztec Row · Berners Road
London N1 0PW

www. harvill.com

1 3 5 7 9 8 6 4 2

A CIP catalogue record for this book
is available from the British Library

The publisher gratefully acknowledges the financial support of
the Kunstsektion of the Austrian Bundeskanzleramt towards
the publication of this book in English

ISBN 1 86046 676 1

Designed and typeset in Bauer Bodoni at
Libanus Press, Marlborough, Wiltshire

Printed and bound in Great Britain by Butler & Tanner Ltd
at Selwood Printing, Burgess Hill

||||||| THE CONTEST |||||||

| 1 |

"A woman poisoned her husband in the suburb of Simmering last week. She added enough cyanide to his breakfast coffee to kill a dozen bulls. It is reported that the man had bullied and browbeaten her for years before she resolved on this counter-measure. Be that as it may, the poor woman could have settled things in a less drastic manner had she learnt to handle her emotions in time."

Thus wrote chess master Georg Hummel in his column in the *Neue Freie Presse* on the day in January 1910 when Emanuel Lasker of Germany and his Austrian challenger Carl Haffner were to play the first game of the world chess championship in Vienna. Hummel was a good journalist. Many people regarded chess as a passion peculiar to scrawny civil servants and artful Jews, and even more tedious than a championship for stamp collectors or crocheters of antimacassars. Hummel stopped at nothing in his efforts to popularize the game with ordinary readers, devising headlines sufficiently sensational to suggest that they had opened the local news section by mistake. He brazenly concocted anecdotes about leading players and drew cogent comparisons between chess and arm-wrestling, painting, tarot-playing – even waltzing. He enticed his readers by making bold and disingenuous statements that were deliberately false.

"I have often pointed out in this column," his piece on the Simmering murder continued, "that nothing is more conducive to mental equilibrium than chess. Has anyone ever heard of an act of violence occurring among the chess fraternity? Chess players are averse to such childishness because they can hold their nerves in check and use the board to protest against the tribulations of our age.

"Let no one imagine, however, that chess players refrain from endeavouring to spite their opponents: the most blood-thirsty prize-fighter – and I say this in all seriousness – is an amiable soul compared to most leading chess players of the present day. World Champion Lasker dispatches his opponents with unparalleled ferocity, and I need waste no words on the pugnacious qualities of Messrs Tarrasch, Janowski, Marshall and associates. Our own Carl Haffner comports himself like a lamb beside them. He plays in a calm and unassuming manner that perfectly matches his temperament. He abstains from daredevil attacks and ill-considered manœuvres. It is as if he's trying to tell his opponent: 'Beat me if you can!' He's the most outstanding representative of the Viennese chess school. In my submission, Carl Haffner is the finest defensive player in the world. He draws a lot of games, I grant you, but it requires the strength of a giant, a genius, to defeat him. Whether or not the mighty Lasker is capable of so doing, we shall discover in the days to come. He and our Viennese master are contesting the world championship at the Vienna Chess Club (No. 2 Wallnerstrasse, Vienna 1). Personally, I do not believe that Lasker will succeed in winning even one of their ten championship games. Why not? Because geniuses do not exist. Not even I, Georg Hummel, am one such."

[4]

Hummel, who was breakfasting at the Marienbrücke Café, perused these lines with satisfaction. It often happened that a compositor ignorant of chess made arbitrary corrections, inserted preposterous subheadings, or spoilt the article in some other way. Today's column had got through unscathed.Hummel rubbed his hands. It was a successful article, he thought, and should bring people flocking to the event in droves.

Hummel ordered a brandy to settle his digestion and unbuttoned the waistcoat over his paunch. He almost bit the end off his Virginia cigar at the prospect of the championship. Although he claimed the credit for having discovered young Haffner's talent, he felt more nervous than he had ever done before sitting down at the chessboard himself. Oblivious of the noises from the street and the comings and goings in the café, which was steadily filling up with people, he kept glancing at his watch to see if it was time to set off to Wallnerstrasse. Anxious not to miss any of the preliminaries, he leafed through the newspapers without even digesting the headlines. Now and then he nodded to one of the café's regulars. Chess master Weiss hurried over to talk shop about Haffner's prospects, his eyes alight with excitement, but was brusquely rebuffed. "Go away! I'm not sharing anything with you – not my table, and certainly not my state of nerves!" At which, Weiss retired with a smile and the perspiring Hummel ordered two more brandies, one of which he sent over to Weiss's table. Weiss raised the glass in acknowledgement. The head waiter was startled to see Hummel stick out his tongue at Weiss, like an outsize frog.

Hugo Fähndrich, Haffner's second, put his head round the door but failed to see Hummel waving and hurried out again. Hummel sank back in his chair. He would have welcomed

Fähndrich joining him at his table because he was, so to speak, a fellow conspirator.

Hummel was plagued by the feeling that the entire café was talking of nothing but the contest. When the head waiter, who usually presided over the establishment with complete discretion, inquired how Haffner was, he rose to his feet. "Really, sir," he snapped, "you're enough to drive one mad!" Inaudibly, he added, "He'll be squatting on the lavatory, what else?" He paid and repaired to the Vienna Chess Club on foot.

Carl Haffner wasn't squatting on the lavatory at all; he was visiting his half-sister, Lina Bauer, who had spent the morning buying newspapers with what remained of her housekeeping money after paying the baker a substantial sum for various breakfast delicacies.

"Are you listening, Carl? It says here: 'Today, the king of chess players, Emanuel Lasker, meets the great Viennese master, Carl Haffner, winner of major tournaments and editor of the *Deutsche Schachzeitung*. Although Lasker must be considered favourite, he has a hard task ahead of him. No one can defend as tenaciously as the likeable Haffner.'"

Carl made a jocular attempt to distract Lina's attention from the newspapers. He praised the delicacies she had bought, even though his hunger had been appeased by a single bread roll. It wasn't simply that he wanted to leave the baker's fine fare for her to enjoy; he wouldn't have ventured to touch it in any case. But Lina didn't notice. She was so bedazzled by the newspaper comments, she even forgot to be her usual solicitous self.

"Aren't you excited, then?" she asked.

Of course he was excited. But ever since entering her warm, impeccably neat apartment, which always smelt of lavender, wax polish and freshly ironed laundry – ever since he had entered it that morning attired in his best suit, the sight of Lina had relegated thoughts of the contest to the back of his mind. In character, Lina resembled the kind of soft, simple melody one hums while strolling across a meadow in summer, wholly in thrall to the breeze and the scent of grass. Haste and raised voices were alien to her. When she flitted through the apartment in her housecoat, silent as a shadow, each of her movements was like a meek apology for her own existence. She completely subordinated her wishes to the welfare of others; or, to be more precise, the welfare of others was her most intimate concern. It gladdened Carl's heart to see her so engrossed in the newspapers. He was long accustomed to seeing his name in print, and even, on occasion, his photograph. Although it was fundamentally abhorrent to him, he could not be ungrateful if it gave her so much pleasure.

She played his favourite piece on the piano before he left, but she declined to go with him. If Lina sat quietly in a corner during a tournament, Carl felt obliged to entertain her, and it spoilt his concentration.

The sun was shining in a cloudless sky, the air was cold and clear, the roadway carpeted with snow. The game was due to start at five o'clock. Carl had been invited to the chess club at two. His lodgings had been unheated for weeks, so it would have been unwise to spend the intervening period there. He walked the streets at random. He did not have enough money for a coffee, and lunch was out of the question. From time to time he crept into a café and absorbed a little warmth in the chess room until, sooner or later, the waiter came to take his order. For all that, spontaneous applause greeted him wherever he went.

[7]

People crowded round, wished him luck and asked what he would like to eat and drink. Carl had to be unusually firm, by his standards. He got away only by pleading that he had to prepare for the game in peace. Hungry though he was, he could not bring himself to accept the hospitality of others; to him, that seemed tantamount to taking the bread out their mouths.

The long walk drove the chill from his limbs. He halted abruptly on the corner of the street in which the Vienna Chess Club was situated. Milling around outside the building were at least a hundred people with a brace of mounted policemen looming over them. A demonstration, thought Carl, and turned on his heel. There was time to spare before the inaugural speeches.

In a nearby park he brushed the snow off a bench and sat down. He suddenly felt sick with excitement. The importance of the forthcoming match was sinking in. Lasker had now been world champion for sixteen years. Not once had he even come close to losing his title – indeed, he had never once been behind on points. Lasker was a scholar, mathematician and philosopher. Every first-class chess player knew his book, *The Philosophy of Struggle*. Who was he, Carl Haffner, to challenge such a man? He could boast a few prizes and one or two drawn matches. He had also beaten Janowski six years ago. Now he was pitting himself against Lasker. It was his task to defeat the world champion in a ten-game series – one in which he, being the challenger, would have to lead by at least one game. In the event of a tie, Lasker would retain the title. Such were the German champion's conditions.

Carl buried his face in his hands and writhed convulsively on the bench. All at once, he felt almost physically tormented by the fear of losing this contest. He prayed he wouldn't lose a single game. As far as he was concerned, every game could end in a draw. Lasker was welcome to remain world champion as long as he himself did not sustain a single defeat.

He trudged back to the Vienna Chess Club. When he embarked on a game, he scarcely cared whether he won or drew. Defeats he found hard to endure. They made him feel puny and helpless – unworthy to shake his opponent's hand.

The crowd failed to notice Carl until he was already in its midst. Then, having been recognized, he was suddenly surrounded by a group of enthusiasts. They yelled salutations in his ear, slapped him on the back, alarmed him with their jostling and chanted "Haffner, Haffner!" The mounted police-men tried to restore order. Carl had never heard such a din in his life. His feet lost contact with the ground, but it was impos-sible to fall over in such a crush. He thought he would suffocate, and he could not locate the entrance to the club. People made to lift him onto their shoulders. At that moment, Fähndrich and Wolf, a wiry local chess master, elbowed their way through the crowd. Linking arms with Carl, they forged a path to the door. But conditions inside the club were just as chaotic. People stood on chairs, shouting and applauding. Carl's escorts took ten minutes to cover the fifteen yards to the inner room in which the organizers of the contest had barricaded themselves.

"Why didn't you use the rear entrance?" Fähndrich asked, when they had succeeded, after a brief scrimmage, in locking the door.

"I don't suppose he was prepared for this," said Arnand Mandl, president of the Vienna Chess Club. "We weren't either. Hummel puts the crowd at three hundred, and it's growing by the minute."

Baron von Rothschild, Europe's wealthiest man and Austria-Hungary's leading chess patron, shook Carl's hand. "Well, how does it feel to be a hero?"

Carl shifted to and fro on the chair that had been brought for him. He found Rothschild's choice of words as upsetting and embarrassing as the rest of the hullabaloo. He asked for a glass of water. That was when he first caught sight of his opponent. Lasker was seated beside the window, one elbow propped comfortably on the sill, his fingers drumming on the pane, his dark, hawk-like eyes regarding Carl intently. Lasker's customary mode of dress was notable for its casualness. Today he was wearing an ill-fitting suit, but he had at least pinned the clasp of some order to his lapel. If one discounted the drumming fingers, his serene and lofty manner appeared to suggest that all the arrangements, seating included, were his own work. He smiled at Carl, who rose, shook hands, and apologized for his apparent discourtesy.

President Mandl ascertained that all the contest's prime movers were now assembled. The pandemonium outside was still as deafening, so he had to deliver his inaugural address in a stentorian voice. Rothschild's address came next, and other officials took advantage of the occasion to speak. Carl heard none of their flowery phrases. His mind was afloat in that amorphous realm for which the term concentration is a wholly inadequate description. More than the mere focusing of all mental forces, it amounted to self-contemplation. They had to call Carl three times to come and draw lots for who should play with the white pieces in the first game. Meanwhile, Lasker seemed quite calm. He, too, addressed the gathering. He underlined the importance of the event, complimented his opponent, and thanked the organizers. But Carl heard none of this either.

That concluded the ceremonial part of the proceedings. Some of those present withdrew to set up demonstration boards in the crowded hall. These boards, which were the size of blackboards and fulfilled a similar function, would enable a number of selected masters to comment on every move for the public's benefit and assess the players' relative chances. At once, the din outside subsided a little.

A buffet was served in the committee room. Lasker did little justice to the rolls and sparkling wine on the grounds that digestive activity impaired his mental processes. Carl was too shy to help himself from the silver salvers. He ate two rolls, and even those had to be pressed on him by Fähndrich: "You're as white as a sheet. Here, eat, you simply must!" He only sipped his wine. His hunger had vanished. The clink of glasses, the excited murmurs, the club secretaries and board setters, the journalists who fawned their way across the room and disappeared again, the scrape of shoes, the isolated, feverish exclamations, Fähndrich's resonant baritone – all these were shadows in a dream-world in which Carl's senses were merely birds of passage. True reality subsisted deep within himself alone. That was where his personality, reduced to its very own, innermost essence, would now encounter Lasker's. Truth is inherent in games between masters, Lasker used to say, and nothing can be hidden on the board: as a human being, each player is stripped naked.

Carl must have been crazy to agree to a contest with such a man.

They were to play in a separate room to which only the seconds, the arbiter and a few privileged persons had access. President Mandl requested the opponents to show themselves in public beforehand. Lasker readily consented. Head erect, he emerged from the door of the committee room and thanked the applauding spectators for their interest. Carl took some persuading. He fiddled with his tie and tweaked his moustache before coming out and waving to the crowd, simultaneously praying that his legs wouldn't give way. Rhythmical chanting and stamping filled the air until President Mandl called for silence: even though the masters would be playing in a side room, he said, nothing must be permitted to disturb their concentration. He was about to say more, but Baron von Rothschild smilingly tugged at his sleeve. The time had come.

Relieved that the rhetoric was over, Carl hurried along the handsome strip of carpet that led to the match room. The arbiter read out the rules governing time limits, wished both contestants luck, and started Carl's clock. Having shaken hands with Lasker over the board, Carl opened with his king's pawn. At that moment, someone came storming into the room.

"Stop! One moment!" called the unknown man. "I need a photograph!"

The seconds prepared to hurl themselves at the intruder. Was he mad? wasn't he familiar with chess etiquette? This was a world championship, after all! The man stood his ground precisely because it *was* a world championship. He didn't care whether the title in dispute was for chess, nose-picking, or long-distance spitting; he wanted to take his photograph. He identified himself as Rainer Lothar of the Vienna Press Agency.

The arbiter shook his head irresolutely when informed of this. The agency carried a lot of weight . . . Would they mind?

With a laugh, Lasker pronounced himself willing to be photographed, and Carl raised no objection either. Smiling superciliously, Rainer Lothar set up his camera, ordered the officials and players into position, and squeezed the bulb. A stench of sulphur filled the room. The photographer handed out some business cards and departed. The seconds and the arbiter milled around in confusion for no reason at all. Only when peace was restored did Carl notice that the reporter's incursion had made him forget to stop his clock and thus set Lasker's in motion. He had lost fifteen minutes' thinking time, but he refrained from lodging a protest.

Both men played their openings with consummate ease. All such moves had long been familiar to both of them, and neither needed a moment's thought before responding to his opponent. Lasker was the first to deviate from the path of theory. Carl pondered this development. Lasker lit a cigar and stared at the top of Carl's head.

What an odd fellow he was, this Haffner: so nervous on entering the chess club, he could hardly stay on his feet. He had not uttered a word during the opening ceremony. A big crowd had applauded him, and he had looked as if he wanted to creep under the carpet. Finally, he'd let a reporter cheat him out of thinking time. Incredible that such a character should be playing chess for the supreme title. Equally incredible was the way he'd sat there, firm as a rock, since the game began. He radiated an assurance that wasn't in character. The man played chess with his entire self, not just with his brain. But character wasn't a mutable state like mood. Haffner's ambivalence required to be understood. Then he could be defeated.

This was their seventh encounter to date. Lasker had won three games, three had been drawn, and the Austrian had decided one duel in his favour at Cambridge Springs in 1904. The mild-mannered man wasn't to be underestimated, nor was he genuinely dangerous, thought Lasker, but it would pay to be careful.

In the smoking room, chess masters and experts stood beside the demonstration boards and in quiet corners, speculating on the outcome of the contest. Few of them fancied the challenger's chances. Even a narrow defeat by six games to four, for example, would have been accounted a major success on Haffner's part. Most people forecast seven to three or eight to two. Hummel alone was convinced that Haffner would win. "He'll never beat Haffner," he kept saying. "Haffner will win at least one game or possibly two, I guarantee you, but Lasker won't win a single one. Haffner is the next world champion!"

Hummel bet old Julius Thirring five hundred crowns that Haffner would win. "Anyone who doesn't bet on Haffner is a heel!" he cried. "Where are all the optimists?"

Reassuring news emanated from the playing room. Neither man was taking any chances, and neither could detect a chink in the other's armour. Haffner had settled into his stride. After four hours the game was adjourned according to plan. Neither man was in the ascendant. The world champion availed himself of his right to request a break, so the game was set to resume in two days' time.

Carl left the club by the back door. Not even his second noticed his absence until too late. He walked home alone through the darkness. The stone walls of his shabby apartment looked glacial. He slept in his clothes, dreaming of positions and strategic plans.

The size of the crowd had not, of course, been solely attributable to Hummel's article. Nearly every newspaper devoted space to the event; indeed, in some cases the world championship ousted even the Simmering poisoning from the headlines.

Many newspapers, in which chess had hitherto been assigned a minor role, now engaged well-known players to contribute a chess column. Efforts were made on all sides to obtain statements from the two opponents. Lasker answered any questions put to him and wrote articles in return for handsome fees, whereas no one managed to elicit a comment from Haffner. Even his whereabouts were unknown. He wasn't at home. One particularly ambitious reporter called on his mother and on Lina Bauer, his half-sister, but to no avail. The Viennese master's conviction that it behoved him to play hide-and-seek with the press was privately deplored as affectation by journalists to whom chess was usually a closed book.

Meantime, Hummel continued to spur Carl on by drumming up public support in the *Neue Freie Presse*. The adjourned game hung in the balance, he reported. This was the most rational and, in all probability, the only objective statement in his article. He did not shrink from comparing Carl Haffner to the biblical David who had overcome Goliath. He invoked the memory of Radetzky and Prince Eugene. In martial language, he called on the Viennese to support one of their own, and, in conjunction with more moderate colleagues, he succeeded. Spectators assembled for the resumption of the game in even greater numbers, and this time the police cordon kept the crowd under control.

Lasker had turned up long before Carl. The rear entrance was also watched over by reporters. Carl failed to elbow them aside, even though his appearance in the match room was overdue. Once again, it was Fähndrich who rescued him from his predicament. Carl was out of breath when he took his place at the board. The arbiter opened the envelope containing Lasker's sealed move. The move was made and Carl's clock started. There followed a swift exchange of pieces. Lasker subsided into a brown study. He had clearly been expecting the game to take a different turn.

Carl had spent most of the previous day roaming the streets. Awakened by the cold after only a few hours' sleep, he saw frost flowers creeping up his window. The pangs of hunger he had suppressed while playing returned to torment him. He could not even wash because the tap on the landing was frozen. A walk would warm him up, he thought. He debated whether to go and see Lina or his mother, but it was still too early for that. He felt weak and dizzy by the time he had wandered the streets for an hour or two. He hadn't the strength to devote due attention to Lina or his mother, and he had no wish to seem rude. Instead, he knocked on the door of the Vienna Chess Club, where a platoon of cleaning women was busy removing all traces of yesterday's proceedings from the main hall. Exhausted after walking so far on an empty stomach, Carl asked the club secretary's permission to lie down for a while in the rest-room. A surprise awaited him when he awoke: a bank messenger had delivered his fee for editing the *Deutsche Schachzeitung* to the secretary's office. After having a light supper at an inn, he returned home late. The reporter who had obtained interviews with Lina and his mother had long since quit his post outside Carl's lodgings.

At the demonstration boards, speculation was rife. What did Lasker's hesitation signify? Was the world champion in difficulties? Word of his next move came through, followed at once by Haffner's response. After a few more moves, chess master Albin announced that the challenger had gained a slight advantage. This news aroused great enthusiasm. Civil servants and senior army officers – men who had played less than half a dozen games of chess in their lives – climbed on their chairs and applauded. After another few moves the masters at the demonstration boards were shuffling from foot to foot. Haffner had one more pawn than Lasker, but was his ascendancy sufficient? wasn't his position too hazardous? No one, neither Albin nor any of the other commentators, dared proclaim the possibility of a Haffner victory. It was as if they feared that a precipitate announcement would influence the Austrian contender's fate to his disadvantage.

The general public were undeceived. Haffner was winning, it was said, at first only in the clouds of cigar smoke in which the masters wreathed themselves, then at the coffee tables and in the lobby, and finally outside in the street. Anyone who assumed that people would cheer all the louder was disappointed. Now, if someone stirred his coffee, the entire hall heard the tinkle of the spoon. In the street, where a demonstration board had also been set up, the crowd neither stirred nor uttered a sound. Inside the main hall, eyes flickered from the boards to the door through which the messenger bearing the next move would come.

Hummel, seated in the hall at a table specially reserved for him, kept everyone at arm's length. He sat there, one hand cupping his chin, the other clutching the handkerchief with which he occasionally dabbed his moist forehead. His eyes were fixed on the demonstration board. He would sooner have gone inside and watched the players in person than be dependent on the messenger – he was authorized to enter the playing room, after all – but suspense had paralysed him. It kept him glued to his chair like everyone else in the hall.

Looking at the rapt faces around him, Hummel understood.

It didn't matter to these people whether or not the world title came to Vienna. That was a gratifying secondary prospect, admittedly, but chess wasn't the issue here. To most of the onlookers, the Ruy Lopez and the Queen's Gambit Declined meant as little as the philosophy that underlay a particular system of play. Some of them knew little more about chess than the way the pieces moved, and many regarded the game as something of a universal mystery. So what had brought them here? The contest alone. How had the photographer put it? He didn't care whether this was a chess match or a nose-picking competition. The same went for those now gazing at the demonstration boards as if intent on an oracle. Their concern was the contest itself: victory or defeat, excitement, and – above all – a decision. The nature of the weapons employed was of secondary importance. These people wanted to watch, at no personal risk, a process to which they themselves were involuntarily subject every day. Quite unlike the conflicts of daily life, this was a contest based on known rules and clear-cut patterns of movement. In life you seldom knew whether or not you won, nor did you know who lay behind the rules of the game. That was the worst part.

Hummel noticed that the people round him had risen to their feet. "What is it?" he called, hurrying over to the demonstration board.

"Adjourned," said Albin.

"Another adjournment? Damn Lasker's conditions! This is chess by instalments."

Albin shrugged. "Nothing to be done. Play will resume in ninety minutes."

Hummel squeezed Albin's arm and set off in search of Carl. He found him in the lobby, surrounded by some masters, but untroubled by ordinary spectators. Carl made a relaxed impression. Looking natural and self-assured, he responded amiably to every question he was asked about possible variations. It went without saying that everyone wanted to know his assessment of the state of play. He said he was confident of being able to hold his opponent to a draw.

"What do you mean, a draw? You're going to win!"

Carl took Hummel's hand. "My dear sir," he said, "you yourself might well contrive to win this game. Positions of this kind are your forte. I shall have to bide my time."

Hummel and several others bombarded him with suggested variations. Carl involuntarily retreated a step. He apologized for having to desert them, but he wanted to take a turn in the fresh air. The masters wished him luck, then hurried to the table at which Weiss and Wolf were analysing the adjourned position. Fähndrich, who appeared some moments later bearing a snack for his protégé, asked where he had got to. At the door he bumped into a woman who caught him by the arm and inquired the whereabouts of Carl Haffner.

"When will he be back? Can someone take me to him?"

Fähndrich scanned the hall. He pointed out Mandl's grey head. "That man there – he's the president. Excuse me."

Mandl, who was making his way across the room as if personally hosting a ball, raised his glass to various distinguished visitors as he went. He looked pleasurably surprised when the woman walked up to him. "My dear lady," he said, "you're the first member of the fair sex to grace this contest with her presence."

"So? Are you going to put me on display?"

Mandl stiffened. The woman looked him boldly in the eye and smiled. "Don't be angry, Herr President – that is your title, isn't it?" Thoroughly flustered, Mandl inclined his head. "Except that I don't have much time for such falderals," she went on. "My name is Feiertanz. I'm here because I'm anxious to meet Carl Haffner, the chess player. I was told you could introduce me to him."

Mandl told her his name. He wasn't only in a position to introduce her to Herr Haffner but would be delighted to do so. Was she an admirer of his? Would she care for some refreshment? Frau Feiertanz answered both questions in the negative, so he conducted her to the match room, where he found her a chair and obtained special permission from the arbiter for her to watch the game.

On the way back to the hall Mandl wondered who the woman was and what she wanted with Haffner. Although a trifle too tall and skinny for his taste and not very smartly dressed, she did possess natural good looks and was undeniably charming. Her socially self-assured manner he put down to coquetry. There was something about her that marked her out from others of her sex. It was unusual for a woman to roam around without an escort, especially at this hour of the night. A prostitute, Mandl surmised, or an actress. Slightly deranged as well, perhaps.

He had no opportunity to introduce Frau Feiertanz to Carl before the game resumed. Carl turned up at the very last moment and could not be disturbed, but the woman could think herself lucky to have obtained a seat in the inner sanctum. Every chair in the main hall was taken once again, and dozens of people shivered outside in front of the torchlit demonstration boards. For the umpteenth time, Baron von Rothschild had to telephone his tarot partner, the Vienna police chief, to prevent his men from clearing the street.

Lasker lost a second pawn. The commentators warned against premature rejoicing: the move was a carefully considered – indeed, brilliant – sacrifice made by Lasker in order to save the game. The hall did not share this opinion. Overexcited laymen insisted on the infallibility of their rule of thumb, which laid it down that a two-pawn advantage augured certain victory. A party of young cavalry officers, attracted to the club in their exuberance following hours of brandy-drinking in sundry taverns, toasted Haffner's victory in champagne in the lobby. Barely able to tell the difference between chess and draughts, they believed that by winning this game Haffner would secure the world championship for the Emperor. They made no secret of their displeasure on hearing that he had accepted a draw. Glasses splintered beneath their boots, bottles shattered against the wall, a table and two chairs were smashed, and, before the merry band marched out of the club, one or two innocent bystanders got boxed on the ear in passing.

Mandl was prevented from introducing Frau Feiertanz to Carl immediately after the game by the crowd that poured into the playing room. He entrusted her to old Thirring and elbowed his way over to the table, only to return looking abashed: Carl had escaped by way of the back door, he reported. Perhaps Fähndrich, who was looking for him in the street, would manage to coax him back. With a smile, Frau Feiertanz absolved Mandl from all blame. Mandl, having ordered coffee and apfelstrudel to pass the time, begged leave to inquire the nature of her interest in Carl Haffner.

2

Rudolph Haffner, Carl's grandfather, had left Königsberg for Vienna in the third decade of the previous century. His father Siegfried, an ambitious, enterprising draper, did well enough in business to be able to send his son to a private tutor. Rudolph was destined to become a physician, but he thought himself unsuited to a medical career. Instead, he misused the books in his father's parlour – by reading them. Goethe he found boring and Shakespeare, at his bloodiest, entertaining, Kotzebue he revered as a great man. But his true mentors were those popular dramatists whose comedies were performed on the Austrian stage. Rudolph himself wrote stories and comic dialogues which he read aloud to his mother, who had no patience with her husband's commercial ambition, but sympathized with her son's secret passion. True, she complained that his writing was just another way of evading the important things in life. Privately, however, she told herself that humour had certain advantages over dour determination, so she covered for her son whenever possible.

Six months after his final examinations she could help him no longer. Although Siegfried Haffner's mind had long been made up, he convened the family council for form's sake.

The younger children were sent to bed, and Rudolph, stationed outside the door, waited for the conference to end. Before long his mother, looking flushed, summoned him into the room.

"You have received an education," said the draper, "such as any father in the city would wish for his son. You have not been harshly treated. You have had freedom as well as obligations." He glanced at his brother Wilhelm, a heavy drinker, who nodded approvingly. "I have granted you several months in which to relax after your examinations. Whether you have made the most of that time, I cannot tell. In any event, you leave here the day after tomorrow."

Rudolph looked startled. His mother went out, slamming the door behind her.

"You will study medicine in Vienna. The University of Vienna has the best reputation. You will write to me once a week, keeping me informed of your studies and your personal welfare. The vacations you will spend here. Provided you do well, I shall support you financially."

Rudolph got drunk in the stagecoach for the first and only time in his life. After two hours he took some writing paper from his hand baggage. "Dear Father," he wrote. "My first anatomy class was a great success. The hall we were in was cold and stank abominably. The abdomen was explained to us with the aid of beggar who had starved to death. The professor slit open his cadaver and removed a slimy, bloody lump which he told us was the liver. Be sure to inform Uncle Wilhelm that a drunkard's liver is a very fine sight. Tomorrow the professor will show us the brain. I am well. Best regards from your son Rudolph."

By the time he staggered off the coach in Vienna, after the

long journey south, there were fifty-two such letters in his case.

Rudolph rented a room from a major's elderly widow. He left there early every morning and spent the day walking the streets and frequenting coffee houses and theatres. When his father stopped sending him money he earned a pittance by performing his comic sketches in wine gardens. Through this he got to know other artistes, one of whom secured him his first engagement. The Karltheater was looking for a librettist, and an actor of his acquaintance advised him to apply for the post. Rudolph, who secretly felt unequal to such a task, shook his head, but the actor took his comic sketches and his first play to the manager of the Karltheater. Rudolph was engaged, and it wasn't long before his own comedies were being staged.

Success wrought a change in Rudolph. He rented an apartment and seldom went out any more. It was unseemly, he thought, for a playwright to roam the streets or fritter away his time in coffee houses. With a portentous air, he had himself measured for suits by the city's finest tailors, whom he paid by instalments. He was a very dilatory debtor, and his Gonzagagasse apartment received many a visit from master tailors demanding payment for first-night outfits.

One day he nearly tripped over a girl slumped on the floor outside the manager's office, a spot where rejected actresses often gave way to disappointment. Whatever it was that prompted him – the girl's dark tresses, her simple gown, her snow-white stockings – he paused to say a few words to her. She jumped up and made to walk off, but he caught hold of her arm. She lowered her eyes and permitted him to stroke her cheek – clumsily, as if brushing a smut off his shirt.

"Come, my girl," he said softly, "things can't be as bad as all that."

She stamped her foot. "My voice is too weak and I move like an old woman. If that isn't bad, what is? Ask the manager – here he comes!"

Rudolph turned and gave the manager an embarrassed nod. Drawing the girl into an alcove where they would be safe from his associates' glances, he introduced himself as the celebrated playwright Rudolph Haffner. Her eyes lit up at this, endearing her to him even more. No theatre had ever rejected one of his students, he assured her. Graciously, he invited the girl – "Your name? Elisabeth?" – to call on him the next day to rehearse a major role.

Elisabeth Gaupmann was the second daughter of a junior civil servant whose wife had died giving birth to her. Exceptionally wilful and flirtatious, even as a child, she was simultaneously pert and coy. She did well at school by virtue of her intelligence, but her tendency to daydream and romanticize, which was more characteristic of her than of other girls of her age, denied her the teacher's commendation. Not that she minded in the least. As Elisabeth saw it, school had no bearing on life. What served her best in real life, she soon discovered, was her smile, her big brown eyes, and the dimples in her cheeks, not the useless knowledge imparted by books.

At eighteen Elisabeth was permitted to accompany Marie, her married sister, to a suburban theatre. It was the most exciting day in her life. The sisters chose their gowns together and helped each other to get ready. A carriage and pair bore them off to the theatre, where Elisabeth had her first sight of the process to which she herself had always aspired: the transformation of one person into another. The leading lady lived an entire lifetime in a few minutes, experienced fear and love, was fêted and mourned.

Elisabeth gave her first performance at breakfast the next morning. With rouge concealing the ravages of a sleepless night, and her feet encased in a pair of her sister's satin shoes, she played the part of a girl who acquaints her irate father with her desire to become an actress. In the event, old Gaupmann merely glanced up from his newspaper – "That's all right with me, carry on!" – and, smilingly, waved her into an empty chair.

Gone was Elisabeth's aversion to the printed page. She borrowed playscripts and memorized all the parts she considered important. Secretly, because she was still convinced that her father disapproved of her ambition, she auditioned for various theatres. All of them turned her down. She wept on her sister's shoulder.

"I don't doubt your talent," Marie said one day, "but violinists spend years at the conservatoire before giving their first recital. It's the same with craftsmen. They have to learn to wield the tools of their trade."

Elisabeth protested at this. What did she have in common with a butcher or a cobbler? Having been rejected by several third-rate theatres after delivering the first few lines, however, she began to think her sister's verdict less unperceptive.

Although Rudolph's salary was only just sufficient to support a small family, he never lost his love of expensive knick-knacks. He had purchased a notebook indistinguishable on the outside from an elaborately engraved cigar box. In this, barely a year after he first met Elisabeth, he wrote: "Today, at half-past four on the morning of 4 April, 1846, my son Adalbert Hermann was born."

Rudolph referred to the notebook as his "chronicle". It was displayed in a locked, glass-fronted cabinet, and one of the maidservant's most important tasks was to dust this cabinet every morning. Rudolph, who opened it only for visitors of distinction, made no secret of his displeasure if they skipped an entry.

There were eleven entries in all. Only four children survived the first few weeks, Adalbert and three girls. The two younger sisters were pallid, lethargic creatures whose favourite occupation consisted in helping their mother with the housework or learning parts for the plays which their father sometimes staged in the parlour. Not so Christine. She also enjoyed play-acting and helping in the house. Unlike Hermine and Natalie, however, she resented the fact that her father devoted more time to Adalbert. Though indulgent towards his daughters, the playwright ruthlessly bullied Adalbert into taking violin lessons, kept him on a tight rein, and supervised him constantly. At the same time, any praise he bestowed on his son was tinged with an affection he never showed the other children. The result was that Christine rampaged around the streets in her brother's clothes and struck fear into all the boys in the neighbourhood. She would appear at supper with grubby hands, shaking the sand out of her hair.

Although her mother did not give up hope of being engaged by a theatre, she received no help from her husband. "My knowledge and experience can't do anything for raw talent," he told Elisabeth. "If I used my connections to secure you an engagement it would harm your reputation, and consequently your career."

In reality, Rudolph was quite amenable to his wife's running the home instead of traipsing round theatres for months out of every year. So Elisabeth did as she used to in the old days, when concealing her proclivities from her father: she made surreptitious sorties from the house to impress her talents on the luminaries of the Viennese theatre.

One day she auditioned at the Burgtheater, whose director wasn'ted for his cold and caustic verdicts. He also regarded the popular theatre as an artistic nightmare conjured into being by the devil himself. Elisabeth was unaware of this when she came on stage, but the director knew who she was. Without even specifying a scene, he called to her from the shadows at the front of the stalls. "Thank you, dear lady! A materfamilias belongs at home with her children. Hers is not a role that has yet been written for the stage. You know whom to consult in that respect. Next!"

Elisabeth was bitterly hurt by this incident, though she suspected that the insult had really been aimed at her husband. It slowly dawned on her that no drama critics would ever mention her name in their columns, and that life with a celebrated playwright wasn't as exciting as she had imagined. Fortunately, she found a scapegoat: her father, who had denied her any form of artistic training.

By degrees, this explanation helped her to forget her ambitions and devote herself to housework. She dismissed the maidservant and drew still closer to Rudolph. One day, she even told her sister not to come visiting any more.

Rudolph Haffner was over fifty when the composer Johann Strauss invited him to write the libretto for his operetta *Die Fledermaus*. Rudolph was well-known and successful, but

Scholz and Nestroy were better-known and more successful still. Failing to grasp the importance of his task, he supplied Strauss with a poor, half-hearted piece of work. His idea for the character of Frosch was all that genuinely satisfied the young composer.

Rudoph's self-confidence was unimpaired by his failure to obtain another commission of such importance. His daughters, who grew up convinced that their father was the greatest playwright of the age, inveighed at school against the critics that ran him down. To Adalbert, on the other hand, his father's status wasn't only a matter of indifference but an incubus. He blamed him for the violin lessons, the theatre-going, the acting lessons, the rehearsals and amateur dramatics at home. The world of greasepaint and scenery was too superficial and boring for him. He could find nothing genuine in it.

On Adalbert's twenty-first birthday his father sent for him. Standing in front of the display cabinet, Rudolph gripped his son by the shoulder.

"Today you're generally considered to have come of age, so this time I've taken the liberty of giving you a special present." He produced a shiny object from his coat pocket. "You'll go your own way, even if it lies in the direction of music rather than writing. Your teacher's latest report was very complimentary."

He handed him the gift. Adalbert turned pale. What he had thought was a silver-mounted cigar case proved to be a book. On the cover he made out some flowing letters blocked in gold. They read: *"The Lovely Ladies of Vienna*, a Comedy. From your brilliant Papa."

"Thank you," said Adalbert. "And now, I'm off to play some

music." He turned on his heel, packed his belongings, and walked out.

Christine always turned up punctually for supper once her brother had left the house. She no longer looked like a street urchin. More than that, she took over her mother's leading role in the home. Adept at managing her father, she readily persuaded him to introduce her to the world of the theatre. It wasn't long before Christine made her first appearance on the Viennese stage. She received six curtain calls, thanks to her father and sisters, and the number of bouquets thrown her was genuinely exceptional for an actress making her debut. No one knew that the most magnificent bouquet of all came from Adalbert. He had slipped into one of the rear stalls at the last minute, and he elbowed his way out through the departing theatre-goers as soon as his family rose to leave.

Adalbert's savings were soon exhausted. He gave his first performances on the violin at about the same time as Christine travelled to Breslau with the Lobe-Theater – but they did not take the form his father had envisaged. To pay the rent, Adalbert competed with cabbies, whistlers and amateur singers for the privilege of busking wine-garden customers into a merry mood in return for a meal and a few groschen. When the clink of the coins in his hat permitted, he would repair to an inn, where he often drank away all his takings. Drinking, which had been banned in his parental home, was very much to his taste.

Adalbert's family did not learn that he had married until some months after the event. Strasser, a painter friend of his father's, happened to enter the establishment where he was performing.

He recognized the playwright's son, although several years had elapsed since Adalbert's departure from Gonzagagasse. The landlord told him what little he knew of the taciturn fiddler: married, no children, an address in the 8th District.

Adalbert received a letter from his father. Couched in affectionate terms, it stated that he had been forgiven, and that everyone was eager to see him. He need not, however, take advantage of the occasion to introduce his wife.

This annoyed Adalbert. What had he done that merited forgiveness? What did his wife's rejection signify? For all that, he wanted to see his family again.

His sisters gave him a chilly reception. Adalbert's heart beat violently as he knocked on the study door. His father was seated at the desk. For a while, nothing could be heard but the scratch of his pen. The top of a maple tree was bending before the wind outside the window. Old Rudolph laid aside his pen, and they embraced.

"You smell like a fishmonger," said the playwright, "but you're looking well."

He gave his son a cursory nod, as though greeting a business associate, and politely indicated a chair. Adalbert asked if he might smoke. His father pushed a table lighter across the desk. From time to time, one of them waved aside the clouds of smoke that floated between them. Finally, Rudolph cleared his throat.

"Are you familiar with the rules of chess?"

"I play badly – hardly at all."

Smiling, Adalbert watched his father swiftly set out a chessboard on the desk. Although he had played a few games at school, he had summoned up no interest in chess thereafter. It surprised him to note how eagerly he now sought the best moves, taking his time. Neither of them looked up when Elisabeth came in bearing coffee and liqueurs. Rudolph wrinkled his nose at the speed with which Adalbert drank.

"You hold your own well," he said after two hours. "But I advise you to attack my king at last. Chasing pawns is futile."

Adalbert stared at the board in bewilderment. When he looked up at his father again, it occurred to him why he had come. He felt the blood rise to his head.

"Maria – my wife – she's expecting a child. If it's a boy, I intend to call him Carl."

Rudolph took a sip of coffee and nodded. "As you wish, but please don't speak to me of your wife. I shall not make that lady's acquaintance until we meet in the hereafter, and I trust your mother and sisters will wait as long."

It took Adalbert a moment to grasp the significance of these words. Then he swept the pieces off the chessboard and stormed out of the room, brushing aside his mother's attempts to stop him. Christine followed him out on to the stairs and called his name. He had forgotten his overcoat.

Adalbert's wife, Maria Reiger, came from Zillingdorf, a small village in Lower Austria. Her parents had hoped that she and her future husband would take over the family inn one day. Although Maria was a quiet, rather listless girl, she persuaded them to let her spend some time in Vienna with her friend Liesl. She longed to be able to go for a walk without bidding good day to everyone she met, and in her dreams the Austrian capital assumed vast dimensions. Half the village accompanied Liesl and Maria to the railway station when they departed one Sunday in summer.

In Vienna the girls took in sewing and waited at table in

various hostelries. Although the conditions in which Maria was living would have seemed unimaginable to her a short while before, they tapped an unsuspected store of vigour and determination. Thoroughly at home in the city within a few weeks, she remained quiet and shy but responsive to all the charms of her new surroundings. Maria was happy to be accountable to no one but herself, and the intervals between her letters to her parents steadily increased. Though compelled to look for work from day to day, she was unworried by this routine struggle.

Adalbert first met Maria at a wine garden. Having laid his fiddle aside, he bowed and asked permission to join the two girls at their table. Maria was neither homely nor particularly pretty. Most men found easy-going Liesl the more attractive, but Adalbert paid court to Maria and married her.

His restlessness undiminished by the birth of young Carl, Adalbert continued to roam the Viennese wine gardens with his fiddle. He would fling open the door late at night and sullenly toss his purse onto his wife's needlework. Maria often gazed out of the window until dawn, waiting for her night-owl of a husband to return. She was robbed of sleep not only by concern for him but by fears for the future. Adalbert seemed permanently depressed, like someone fighting off a disease. Liesl opined that he was suffering from "marriage fever", and that he was still unused to the company of a wife and child. "It happens," she said. "Don't worry."

Adalbert spent far more time on the streets than in taverns. It wasn't his new status that impelled him to roam the city, for he and Maria were bound by close ties of affection. He was tormented by uncertainty about the purpose of his own existence and driven to despair by constant shortage of money.

Sometimes, when his conscience pricked him, he would play with little Carl and take Maria into town. On other remorseful days he invited friends to their home. But before long he would be hurrying through the wide, deserted streets once more, anaesthetizing himself against hunger by chewing on a twig or a quid of old tobacco. His days were cold and sunny.

The ceremonial procession in honour of the imperial couple's silver wedding brought all Vienna out onto the streets. Adalbert's daily flight from reality had taken him to the Prater, where he sighted the leading carriages. He could not help thinking at that moment of his home, of the two basement rooms in which Maria toiled, and of Carl, listening attentively as he played in silence with a handful of pebbles on the floor. All at once he felt so sorry for the little boy that he turned and hurried home.

Carl never forgot that April day he spent in the streets at his father's side. On the way to the Ringstrasse he asked incessant questions about the emperor and empress, whom his imagination equated with the magical monarchs that figured in his mother's fairy tales. He did not fall silent until the leading carriage came into view.

Men in a variety of costumes marched slowly by. Many of them led dogs on leashes, others had bulging sacks on their shoulders, and one was carrying a dead goose. Huge, caparisoned horses trotted past, one of them ridden by a man with a hawk perched on his wrist. Carl heard the crack of a whip. Yes, there she was: the empress! Rumbling along behind a group of dancers came a wagon, its sides festooned with greenery. The empress was seated on a bare board beside the stern-looking driver of the team. Carl had pictured her far more beautiful and more gorgeously attired. Her dress

[34]

looked just like any other woman's. Not only was her hair dishevelled, but she wore no crown. The armed men riding beside the wagon seemed to be laughing at her. Had they taken her prisoner?

Carl started to cry. His father laughed when told the reason. "That isn't the empress," he said. "This is a party of huntsmen with their game wagon, and the woman is their quarry."

Carl stared at the procession uncomprehendingly. Just as he turned to look at his father in disbelief, he heard a crack. The horses harnessed to the wagon reared, the driver stood up on his box and hauled on the reins, the woman whom Carl still thought of as the empress clung to a wooden rail in terror. All at once, the horses shot forwards. The driver fell off, the horses bolted into the crowd. Screams arose from the cloud of dust in which the wagon came to rest.

Carl had the feeling that his father was being drawn to the spot by some outside agency. Stiff and silent, Adalbert pushed his way through the throng. A big circle had formed around the overturned wagon. One man was holding his head, another leaning on a friend as he hobbled away, yet another was kneeling on the ground beside a bundle of bloodstained clothes. Carl felt sure this bundle was the woman from the wagon. He could see her companion more clearly once the dust had settled. A beardless young man, he was fanning the woman with his cap and calling for a doctor. The woman did not stir. The man jumped up and raced madly around the circle of bystanders as if he could recognize a doctor by his cast of feature. Then he pulled himself together and returned to the woman, calling her name and calling for a doctor by turns. All that could be heard was his cracked, despairing voice. The onlookers stood there in tense, expectant silence. Just then, a cry rang out. It was

[35]

an animal sound, but it came from the woman. An old man standing beside Carl said, with an odd smile, "She's past saving You can't help feeling sorry for the youngster."

Carl saw the man with the cap snatch a soldier's rifle from him, run back to the woman, and ram the bayonet into her chest. A groan went up from the spectators. Soldiers in resplendent uniforms hurried over to the youth, who had hurled himself on the woman and was holding her in his arms. The leaves of a massive oak tree could be heard rustling in the wind.

Adalbert never looked for work. Although he was faithful to Maria in the sense that he never made up to other women, he seldom felt affection at the sight of her. He welcomed Maria's presence, but he did not love her.

He had given up reading books. No book could answer the questions that goaded him through the streets and across the bridges of Vienna, the unspoken questions about the meaning and course of life that made him haunt weddings and funerals. Adalbert had the impression that many philosophers wrote books simply to avoid being driven mad by their own uncertainties.

But he continued to feel burdened by a responsibility that sometimes seemed immeasurably great. On such occasions he hurriedly scraped up enough cash to invite some friends to supper. They needed no second bidding, neither Liesl, who changed her male companions with great frequency, nor the Haseks and Lechners, two couples who seemed as carefree as they were impoverished. Maria did more than justice to her mother's culinary tuition, and Adalbert transformed himself into an attentive host. He enjoyed playing games after the meal. Charades and tongue-twisters made him laugh till he doubled up in his chair, and thus, to Maria's annoyance, roused young Carl from his bed.

Adalbert was particularly fond of a game in which one member of the party was blindfolded and some object was removed from the table. When relieved of his blindfold, the player had to name the missing object as quickly as possible.

One night, everyone was in such a festive mood that Carl escaped being sent to bed after supper. His ears glowed as time went by and still he was allowed to sit at table in his knitted jumper and patched trousers. The blindfold game enthralled him. Carl was a quiet, undemanding child, so everyone was surprised at the alacrity with which he begged for a turn with the blindfold. Lechner laughingly tied the black cloth round his head. When it was removed, Carl took a quick look and sang out, "The sugar caster!" Sure enough, Liesl had hidden it under the table.

Beaming delightedly, Carl asked to be blindfolded once more. This time Hasek's cigarette case was missing. Carl had no need to request the blindfold again. In quick succession, he readily detected the disappearance of a newspaper, a candle end, and a singularly inconspicuous glass. Lechner clapped his hands. "Very impressive, Carl. Now let's see how much of an expert you really are. Wait outside the door and we'll change something somewhere in the room – the whole room, you understand?"

Carl pulled on his thick woollen stockings and went out into the dank passage. When he left the apartment on ordinary occasions to fetch coal from the bunker, the mangled, screaming woman and other ghosts were lurking in corners. They could not get at him now.

Lechner's cry of "Ready!" brought him hurrying back into

the living-room. He pointed to a blank space on the wall where a picture had been removed. In quick succession, he spotted the absence of his father's violin case, the coal rake, a bunch of flowers – even the tablecloth, which the cunning grown-ups had removed, leaving the remains of supper in place.

Then came a time when Carl had to restrain his eager legs for longer than before. He darted back into the apartment as soon as Lechner summoned him in.

His smile gave way to a look of bewildered consternation. He could sense quite clearly that something was missing. Shuffling round the room like an old man, he surveyed the walls, scanned the floor, peered at the grown-ups' expectant faces. All of a sudden, the wall clock chimed with the insistence of a church bell.

"Strikes me this wasn't very nice of us," Lechner said. "Poor Carl, it's not your fault – it's too far-fetched." He raised his voice. "And now, let's summon up the Devil . . ."

The heavy curtain, which reached to the floor, bulged, and out stepped a figure with twinkling eyes: Adalbert. Carl buried his face in his hands and sobbed, spun round and ran to his room. His father cradled him in his arms until he went to sleep.

3

Before the second game of the world championship Baron von Rothschild was sent off to play cards with the chief of police and win his permission to install benches in the street outside the Vienna Chess Club. Rothschild duly won. The organizers also provided a hot punch bar and a roast chestnut stall. Four times as many demonstration boards were set up and half the tables removed from the main hall.

Mandl retired to his office once his instructions had been carried out. Contentedly, he lit a cigar. He had even thought of minor details such as reserving Frau Feiertanz a seat in the match room. He was doubly surprised, therefore, when a secretary burst into the office and announced that ructions had already broken out in the hall.

Not a seat remained unoccupied three hours before the game was due to start. New arrivals, many of them not entirely sober, angrily demanded chairs. Scuffles broke out between the seated and the standing. Herr Kolaric, a distinguished academic, refused to give up his chair and got his jacket torn. Mandl came bustling up and ordered the rowdies to leave. They totally ignored him. At his wits' end, he hurried off to see the constables in the street, but they had their orders: what went on inside the club was no concern of theirs. Rothschild's friendship with the chief of police stood the test of another telephone call, and the constables assumed responsibility for keeping order in the hall.

Hummel, seated over a brandy, successfully defended his table with teeth bared. Although he could not help laughing at the sight of Mandl scurrying around in a panic, he deplored the class of people he had enticed to the scene. He was glad if his chess column had lured the public away from wrestling bouts between mountains of flesh, but the way these fellows were behaving . . .

He recalled a letter he had received during the week. The writer, who introduced himself as Colonel Keller, regretted that he was stationed at Linz and, consequently, unable to wish Carl Haffner luck in person; that was why he was doing so at one remove. Although he accepted that Haffner wasn't under his command, the colonel had an order to give him: he must not only trounce his Jewish opponent; when White, he must not, on any account, employ the Jewish opening d4. To open with a two-step by the queen's pawn was a typical mark of craven Jewish decadence; a man of honour, untainted by Jewish blood, always moved his king's pawn first! Such was the precept with which he desired to send the Austrian contender into battle.

Anna Feiertanz was the daughter of an art dealer who period-ically succumbed to an addiction to gambling. Her mother had died young, and her father went to his eternal rest without leaving a single crown. Anna just managed to cover his debts by selling off his stock. Thereafter she kept herself afloat by taking a variety of jobs. She worked as a waitress, fair-copied an author's short stories, was temporarily employed as lady companion to an elderly countess, played walk-on parts, and modelled for artists. The latter occupation she abandoned on discovering that most painters were devoted not only to art but, in equal measure, to feasting their eyes on her naked body. To Anna, nudity was something neutral and natural. She abhorred the hypocrisy of citizens who despised women by day and leered at them in *risqué* cabarets by night. Together with a number of kindred spirits, she founded a nudist club that shocked summer visitors to the banks of the Danube. This landed her in the goal more than once. Flexible though she was by nature, she stubbornly persisted in this activity. Even heavy fines failed to deter her from bathing in the nude. When she was hot she was hot, she told herself. She hadn't come into the world in a corset, after all.

It was a newspaper article that had whetted her interest in Carl Haffner the chess player. She knew little about chess and had no great opinion of the game – in fact all forms of conflict made her feel uneasy. She herself had only once resorted to physical violence. "The sword is man's to wield, so take up arms! When men make war, women should hold their peace!" She had been so infuriated this dig at Bertha von Suttner's pacifist novel, *Lay Down Your Arms*, that she sought out its author, the poet Felix Dahn, and slapped his face.

What sort of man was he, this Carl Haffner? The article stated that he often accepted a draw, even when in a command-ing position, because of his reluctance to hurt an opponent's feelings. This did not accord with Anna's idea of a chess player. Haffner was characterized as someone who "never covets what another person craves". So why did he aspire to the world championship? The article answered this question too: Haffner had not personally challenged his opponent; the Vienna Chess Club had issued the challenge and Lasker had accepted it. If only for his friends' sake, Haffner had felt duty-bound to play.

Anna was looking forward to the evening ahead. She had felt thoroughly at home in the atmosphere of the inner sanctum, where nothing could be heard but the ticking of the clock and the squeak of the arbiter's shoes as he made an occasional circuit of the room. It suited her perfectly that she hadn't been introduced to Haffner right away. This would enable her to observe both players without any preconceptions. Haffner kept his eyes fixed on the board. He betrayed no emotion and never got up, but he didn't look constrained or dejected, just pleasantly preoccupied. Without precisely knowing why, Anna had the impression that he looked upon his opponent as a comrade, if not an elder brother for whom he cherished respect and affection. There was no question of this where his opposite number was concerned. Lasker shifted his chair around, cracked his knuckles, and sometimes rose abruptly to his feet, but he did not budge from the table: he stood staring down at Haffner like a beast stalking its prey.

Accustomed to victory as he was, the world champion found himself facing renewed problems in the second game. Hummel, who was familiar with Haffner's idiosyncrasies at the board, roamed the lobby and announced in a booming voice that he wanted to double his bet. If Haffner could find the time to stroll up and down and chat with the onlookers during play, it meant that he was secretly confident, not only of winning the current game but of mastering his opponent altogether. Lasker, for his part, sat glued to his chair. He bent over the board with tousled hair and an unlit cigar in his right fist.

Then something happened. "Really!" the world champion exclaimed. "This is no way to play!" He tugged at his tie, tossed it away, and undid his shirt collar. Hummel witnessed this incident. "Of course, Haffner's got him by the throat!" he told himself, and left the room once more to join Albin at the demonstration board and tell him of Lasker's outburst.

Mandl was at last able to fulfil his promise to introduce Frau Feiertanz to Haffner. Having done so, he promptly and discreetly withdrew. "About time too!" he whispered to Rothschild. "I mean, have you ever seen him with a woman?" Rothschild nodded. "Twice, no less. In the street. With his mother."

Anna informed Carl point-blank that her only reason for being there was to make his acquaintance. She told him about the newspaper article. Noticing his embarrassment, she momentarily grasped his hand. "I know," she said, "you've other things on your mind at present. We'll speak again after the game – if you're agreeable." Lasker made his move, and Carl hurried back to the board feeling bewildered. Nothing of the kind had ever happened to him before. He hadn't even gathered what the woman expected of him.

This game, too, was adjourned. The room filled with people eager to analyse the course of play with the contestants. Carl would much rather have left by the back door, as before, but this was impossible. He had promised to speak with the woman after the game. He rose, half hoping that Frau Feiertanz had departed in the interim. When he looked around and failed to see her, he felt relieved. Female company unnerved him. He got on far better with men.

Then he heard a woman laugh. Frau Feiertanz was standing with Hummel at the arbiter's table. Hummel beckoned Carl over. He took his leave of Frau Feiertanz and threaded his way through the spectators who were listening to Lasker's analysis. "Splendid creature, that!" he told Carl. "Go on, she's expecting you."

On 16 January the world champion published a piece in the *Neue Freie Presse*:

"Two of the games in the world championship series have been played, and both have ended in draws. Many people, myself included, have been surprised by this. I would comment as follows:

"Haffner favours a style of play that differs entirely from that of my opponents of the last fifteen years. Steinitz, Marshall, Tarrasch and Janowski were all inclined to take the initiative, whereas the Austrian champion's predominant concern is safety. Any undertaking must give promise of sure success before Haffner consents to remove his forces from their base. Not even the prospect of a win can induce him to do otherwise. Haffner has introduced a novel and thoroughly topical problem. How is it possible to defeat a player who greets the promise of success and the threat of an attack with the same sang-froid; who is primarily concerned with his own safety and pursues it with great expertise and, if need be, with great flair and perspicacity? The answer to that question is still unknown. In theory, however, the following statement may be made:

"If, at the right juncture, Haffner's strategy were allied with initiative, the perfect style would have been attained and Haffner would be unbeatable. It is not, however, given to any mortal man to be infallible. A chess player's virtues are only approximations to the ideal. Everyone has a weakness somewhere, notably timidity, excessive audacity, or lack of observation. It will be my task, in the eight remaining games of the championship, to undertake the first attempt to solve the Haffner problem."

One reads of a chess player's "style". Many will question the aptness of that designation. One speaks of style in the case of painters and writers, but chess players? Well, a chess master devotes as much energy and imagination to every move as a writer to every word of every sentence. Confronting one another over the chessboard are two stylistic tendencies, two systems, two philosophies. Once the opening moves have been made, the master selects a plan based on the characteristics of the position that has come into being. No master deviates from his plan unless his opponent substantially alters that position. One player may possess an exceptional talent for accumulating minor advantages and combining them in such a way as to decide a game in his favour; another have a capacity for working out combinations of moves that surpass his opponent's in depth and extent. One may be noted for his peculiarly aggressive play; another will wait for his opponent to attack. Every true master has a style of his own. A musician doesn't invent songs, he composes them. A writer doesn't simply write books, he puts them together. Similarly, a great chess master doesn't play games, he constructs them.

Viewed thus, chess displays some thoroughly artistic features. Unhappily for the chess artist, however, his work of art – if so it may be termed – requires the participation of two persons. Some chess masters will fly off the handle if an opponent plays badly.

Very few people are capable of appreciating the beauty of a

perfectly constructed game of chess. Generally speaking, the ordinary player is quite unable to grasp why one master has defeated another. If chess masters' errors were living creatures, they would be visible only under a microscope, and the errors of the greatest masters cannot be countered by technique alone. In any generation of grandmasters there are two at most, or perhaps only one, who can see at a glance what other grandmasters would fail to detect in a month. Those are the world champions – men whose cerebral processes are not only uncanny but, as a rule, highly specialized. Playing chess at world championship level entails an ability to penetrate infinitely far into a microcosm while retaining an overview of the great totality.

Not even his natural courtesy prevented Carl Haffner from devoting the rest of the evening to an analysis of the second game of the championship instead of spending it with Anna. He had arranged to meet her on the morrow of the third game. This passed off without incident and ended in another draw. But Lasker was soon to discover that his opponent presented far more of a problem than he could ever have imagined.

| 4 |

When a teacher at Carl's old school was ill, another teacher stood in for him. At his new school, Carl discovered, such situations were handled differently. The last two lessons of the day were cancelled because of a teacher's indisposition, and the boys were allowed to go home.

Carl's mother usually waited for him at the school gates. Today, of course, when he trudged out into the year's first flurry of snow in his thin jacket, she wasn't there. He walked up and down for a while, wondering what to do. He was in two minds: should he wait at the entrance or take the plunge and walk home alone? He had still not decided when some of his new classmates came skipping past.

"What's the matter, did your mother catch the teacher's cold?"

Franz, the sturdy, broad-shouldered boy who ruled the roost in class, planted himself in front of Carl. "Your name's Carl, isn't it? Come along with us. Then, when you get home, you can show your father the kind of things you're learning at school."

Everyone laughed. "Leave him be," called a voice. "He's a wet blanket."

Franz took hold of Carl's hand. Carl snatched it away, but he picked up his school bag and trailed after the others.

For the first few yards he wondered if he was breaking a rule by going on this jaunt, which was taking him in the opposite direction to his home. Then curiosity overcame his misgivings. Besides, he was glad not to be the butt of coarse sallies, as he was in class, or pelted with snowballs. Everyone crowded round Franz, eager to know where they were going, and halted obediently when he raised his hand like a platoon commander on patrol. With a conspiratorial air, he signalled to them to be quiet, then ran across the street and disappeared into a fine new house.

"It belongs to his father," someone said in a low voice.

"No, it doesn't! His father's the janitor. My father knows the family, he said so at supper!"

"His father's rich, I tell you! He owns a lot of houses like that one. I've been there, and his father's a toff – he showed me his pocket watch. Ah, there's Franz!"

Being unfamiliar with this part of town, Carl memorized every building, every tree, so as to be able to retrace his steps later on. After making their way down a side street, across some waste ground, and into a small park, the boys halted at a spot particularly well screened by some bushes laden with snow. First, Franz made sure that no one out for a stroll had strayed into the park despite the wretched weather. He scanned the boys' faces and gave a satisfied nod, as though he considered them all worthy of sharing his secret. Then he reached into his pocket and brought out something wrapped up in a handkerchief.

"Come on, what are you waiting for?" someone said eagerly. "Is it a knife?"

Franz unwrapped the little bundle without a word, and some cigars came to light. There were seven of them, one apiece.

"Zahalis," whispered Franz.

"Not a bad brand."

Carl felt his cheeks turn puce. He didn't want to smoke. His father smoked the odd cigar at home, and the very smell made him queasy, but there wasn'thing for it. Franz handed round the brown cylinders.

When it was Carl's turn to light up, he could not manage it. "You've got to suck, not blow!" cried Franz. Carl took a couple of puffs and blew out the smoke at once. It tasted terribly bitter.

"That's not the way," said one of the boys. "You have to inhale it."

Carl tried. His cigar fell into the snow. The others leapt aside, roaring with laughter, as he vomited. His knees buckled. He was only just over his bout of retching and back on his trembling legs when someone came up with a proven cure for nausea, or so he claimed: he massaged Carl's neck and face with snow until the others' applause subsided. Carl's one desire was to be at home in bed. The shirt was clinging dankly to his body, and his sodden jacket weighed him down. He almost forgot his school bag in his eagerness to be gone. The others sent him on his way with shouts of encouragement. He screwed up his eyes against the snow, which was falling more and more heavily. He had never felt so cold in all his life.

For ten years, Adalbert's relationship with Maria had resembled that of a brother and sister who live under the same roof but seldom exchange a word. Like some solitary stranger, he had been impelled to traverse the Danube bridges by a feeling of unspeakable emptiness. He roamed a city in which one building after another was being erected; a city which, like everything else that met his eye, was growing ever bigger and more incomprehensible. People were flocking from all parts of the empire to the scene of Adalbert's daily wanderings, the place where he played his fiddle and – with increasing frequency – drank to excess. His life seemed to him as meaningless as that of an animal or the emperor. That was what grieved him.

In recent months the hours he spent at home had become fewer still. In the morning he fled from his bed as if compelled to sleep in a coffin. At breakfast he stared into space and drummed on the table. He could hardly bring himself to be civil to his wife any more.

And then he fell in love.

Adalbert awoke with a start. At the sight of Maria, who was bent over her sewing, he had a momentary recurrence of the strangely impersonal affection with which he had eyed her before going to bed. He hurried behind the screen, hurriedly pulled on his clothes, donned his coat and shoes. When he returned from the lavatory, a dark and malodorous cubbyhole along the passage, Maria said, "Anyone would think the bed was on fire."

Adalbert sat down across the table from her. Too hardened a drinker to suffer from hangovers, he had ceased to notice the ache behind his eyes or the deadening of his senses.

Reposing on his plate was a cold boiled potato, and beside it the water jug. For a while he listened to the clatter of horses' hoofs outside the window, humming a popular song with a studiously cheerful air. To underline how innocuous the previous night had been, he proceeded to tell Maria about a conversation he'd had with Samuel Gold at the Gasthaus zum Hirschen. Samuel Gold, a bookseller and journalist, had never set foot inside the Gasthaus zum Hirschen, but Maria had once turned up while he and Adalbert were chatting outside that hostelry. Adalbert recalled that Gold had waxed enthusiastic about the chess column some newspaper had employed him to write.

"Gold is writing about chess in the newspaper these days," said Adalbert. "You should have seen him. Very excited, he was – spent the whole night talking about chess problems. That's what he calls the positions he devises – or 'composes', to use his own term. Each position dictates a logical succession of moves that will enable one player to defeat the other in an especially elegant way." Adalbert took a big swig of water. "Though God knows what's elegant about it," he growled.

He raised his head and looked Maria in the eye. She was crying.

She stuck her needle in the pin-cushion. "Your face is all bloated," she sobbed. "You look like those drunks who lie around in the street day and night. You smell vile, hadn't you noticed? You're oozing rot-gut, sweating schnapps."

He was unable to reply. Her outburst was like a slap in the face, like a long-dreaded but ultimately unexpected form of punishment. He stared at Maria, who did not look away. She continued to gaze at him, eyes blank and mouth wide open in a kind of rictus. After a while she rested her head on the table.

How thin her hair is getting, thought Adalbert. That banished his inertia. He was suddenly assailed by an irresistible urge to explode. He flung his plate at the wall, so hard that the fragments came raining down on the table, and sprang to his feet. His eye fell on an old rocking-chair in which he sometimes read the newspaper. Maria had bought it for him at the very outset of their marriage, out of what she earned from sewing. He picked it up and smashed it against the doorpost. A choking sensation overcame him. Yielding to some deep-seated impulse, he took hold of the door-frame and banged his head against the panels – once, twice, again and again. He shut his eyes.

Maria had witnessed the destruction of the chair without seeking shelter from the flying debris. She had stopped crying and was sitting there impassively, the needlework still on her lap. When Adalbert started banging his head against the door, she discarded her sewing and darted over to him. Catching hold of his waistband, she tried to haul him back. He clung still more tightly to the doorpost and continued to bang away. Let go of me, he thought. Go away, let go of me. Leave me alone.

In his frenzy, he failed at first to notice that his head had ceased to meet any resistance. He opened his eyes.

Carl, holding the door ajar, stared uncomprehendingly at his father's bleeding forehead, at his mother clasping him round the waist from behind, at the blood on his father's face, at the pair of them standing in the doorway. Too cold and weary to make sense of it all, he started to cry.

Adalbert found it just as hard to discern the relationship between himself, his present situation, and his deathly pale, soaking wet son. Where had the boy sprung from at this hour? How had he got into such a state? Bewildered, Adalbert ruffled Carl's hair. Maria let go of him. Without more ado, he set off up the stairs and away from the godforsaken basement apartment, out into the street and away from them both.

After a moment's helpless indecision, Maria pulled herself together. She wasted no more thought on her fleeing husband. Pouncing on Carl, she undressed the boy and wrapped him in a blanket. The hot bath she prepared for him cost her over half their remaining stock of coal.

Carl didn't wait to be interrogated. Trembling with cold and misery, he recounted his adventure. He left nothing out, neither the cigar nor the vomiting. To his surprise, Maria was not angry. She took pity on him, promised that he needn't go to school tomorrow and that he would be better in no time.

Softly, Carl inquired what she and his father had been doing in the doorway earlier on. Had Papa hurt himself? Maria tidied her hair. Kneeling down beside the boy's chair, she tickled him in the ribs. "You know the story of Little Johnny Head-in-Air?" she said. "Well, your father's a Johnny Head-in-Air. He looks left and right and up and down but never straight ahead. That's why he bumps into doors and hits his head on them."

Adalbert trudged through the snow, occasionally shaking his fist at some invisible foe. He'd betrayed himself by hurrying back to the apartment. Some goblin spirit of remorse had prompted him to find out how Carl was faring – the boy had come home in a wretched state, after all. But Maria! He needn't worry, she said, she was quite capable of putting Carl to bed by herself. She'd sent him packing like a supplicant!

His ill humour vanished once he was patting the snow off his coat outside the Gasthaus zum Hirschen. He might have been entering a better world. Stationing himself at the counter, he ordered some coffee and a large schnapps. The proprietress asked about the blood on his forehead. He exchanged a few trivial pleasantries with her. His heart pounded and he turned his head whenever the doorbell tinkled, hoping that it was Leopoldine. Even the gallow's-bird faces of his boon companions and drinking acquaintances were a disappointment.

Adalbert spent hours playing cards with the proprietress and a fellow customer. He won a little money, as he always did at cards, and drank schnapps after schnapps until well after dark. Even when the shutters had long been closed and the door locked and he was the only customer left in the establishment, he continued to hope that Leopoldine would absolve him from having to drink his last schnapps alone. Eventually, he would ask the proprietress to chalk up what he owed, and stagger out into the cold.

Adalbert spent several days of every week like this, steadfastly waiting for Leopoldine and getting drunk meanwhile. When she failed to appear, he poured out his heart to the proprietress. He had no cause to do that on Fridays and Saturdays; on the contrary, those were his red-letter days, because that was when Leopoldine helped behind the bar. She and the proprietress were on close terms, not that they ever said as much. The latter played fairy godmother to the complicated affair between Leopoldine and Adalbert, for whom her hostelry was at once a focal point and a refuge. On Fridays and Saturdays and the few nights Leopoldine could get away, she was not averse to leaving them alone together in the taproom.

So Adalbert had got to know Leopoldine as a customer and a drinker. He did not fall in love with her right away. He knew that she had a boyfriend, a workman named Gustl with whom he had sometimes played cards before she started work at the Gasthaus zum Hirschen. During her first month's employment there, Adalbert regarded Leopoldine merely as a nice young barmaid. In the second month they chatted over the counter about this and that, and he delighted in her warmth and lack of affectation. In the third month it struck him that she was beautiful – extraordinarily so – and that her face reflected her innermost self. All at once, Adalbert felt unin-hibited and alive. There ensued nights of merry-making during which Leopoldine matched him schnapps for schnapps and he entertained the late-stayers with humorous anecdotes.

On one such occasion Leopoldine drew him into the kitchen, where they were safe from the eyes of the roistering regulars. She had a glass of schnapps with her. "Know what I'd like to do most of all?" she asked, straight out.

Adalbert could not speak. He knew that something momentous was about to happen.

She took his hand, cupped the palm, and filled it with schnapps. Inclining her head, she drank the spirits from his hand and dried it with her lips. Then she straightened up, looked him full in the eye, and kissed him. Adalbert thought he was going out of his mind.

At that instant, the world he had spent a lifetime longing to comprehend revealed itself to be a meaningless piece of theatre. In the eyes of this girl, who was little more than twenty years old, he perceived the truth and reality of what he had been seeking. It was the most authentic moment of his life.

Carl was confined to bed with pneumonia for three weeks. Maria had to borrow the money for the doctor from Liesl, who found the time to look after Carl in the afternoons. That was when Maria snatched a few hours' sleep. At night she sat up with Carl, trying to suppress her anxiety by doing some needlework. When Adalbert came blundering into the apartment in the small hours, she would ask him feebly not to make a noise. "How's Carl?" he would growl, opening the door and peering into the darkened room for a while before turning away with a shake of the head. He always retired to bed without another word. Maria praised heaven whenever Carl did not wake up. Quiet was all she wanted from Adalbert these days. In other respects, he was welcome to do as he pleased.

One day, the doctor pronounced Carl recovered. He did, however, add that time alone would tell whether the boy's constitution had been lastingly impaired.

Leopoldine swore that she loved Adalbert, but in the next breath she would say it was a mistake for them to see each other again. She had been going with Gustl for years and could not face leaving him.

Adalbert, on the other hand, was ready to desert Maria and Carl at the drop of a hat. Leopoldine's attitude mystified him. If she loved him so much, why should she be incapable of detaching herself from Gustl? The latter sometimes came to the inn and sat down beside him at the bar, all unwitting. Adalbert was stung by Leopoldine's intimacy with Gustl. It surprised him that she could hide her feelings so well.

Many a time, Adalbert would regard the workman with schnapps-moist eyes and feel convinced that Leopoldine must love him. Gustl was young and sturdy. He laughed a lot, showing his white teeth, was universally friendly, and never seemed depressed. What was he himself in comparison? An ugly, ageing animal.

On other occasions, Adalbert would feel on top of the world. He could clearly discern the workman's natural deficiencies and his inability to give a girl as thoughtful as Leopoldine what he, Adalbert, had to offer her. Gustl was shallow. There was nothing exciting or exceptional about him. He was no match for Adalbert. Adalbert felt that he must fight for Leopoldine – that he must make every conceivable effort to wrest her away from such a man.

Although Adalbert's heart thumped whenever Gustl, with a weary smile, shuffled into the inn in his worn and grimy shoes, his rival's visits were slightly less unwelcome than they had been. He did his best to vie with Gustl in everything. It delighted him to win half a month's wages off the workman at cards and then, with Leopoldine looking on, refuse to take the money. He even competed with him physically. Arm-wrestling was very popular at the Gasthaus zum Hirschen. Adalbert did not take part as a rule, but one night, when Gustl had uncharacteristically drunk too much, Adalbert challenged him to a bout. He wanted to win – he was absolutely determined to do so – and win he did, though he charitably ascribed Gustl's defeat to the exertions of his working day.

Adalbert made special efforts to chat with Gustl at the counter. Leopoldine often joined in these conversations while filling glasses with beer and spirits, and Adalbert's ear was ever alert to the occasions when she and Gustl differed a little on some point or other. Quite imperceptibly, Adalbert schooled the girl in his own opinion of the emperor, of wealth, happiness and morality. He led her on step by step, developing her half-formed ideas until she nodded in agreement and said, yes, that was just what she thought too. It was hardly surprising that Gustl often went home before closing time without waiting for her. He was quite unsuspecting. He believed in

Leopoldine's fidelity as steadfastly as the truest of devotees in the existence of God.

But Adalbert had yet to possess her completely. Although they kissed and fondled one another, Leopoldine could not bring herself to cast off the last shackles of restraint on a bench in the smoky taproom. Adalbert protested that one's emotions should not be denied, and that, besides, kissing alone did not render a person unfaithful. Leopoldine thought otherwise. Even though she looked upon Gustl as a brother who could no longer possess her as a woman, her conscience troubled her more and more. Adalbert, for his part, felt guiltless where Maria was concerned. "I love you," he told Leopoldine, "and love sanctifies everything. It's a sin against love to suppress it."

Adalbert moulded Leopoldine's thoughts and voiced them aloud, but that was why she failed to see him as a person who knew her innermost self. It was the other way round. Although Maria had given Adalbert security, he had never really known her. In Leopoldine he perceived something intrinsically, profoundly familiar to him. She alone knew his language. Her eyes gave promise of something iridescent and unfathomable. This he embraced, rejoicing in his own defencelessness.

One Saturday night they pushed some tables together to lie on. Adalbert was drunker than usual. His vision was blurred, and he felt he was squinting. Leopoldine had drunk just as much. Thick-tongued, she bemoaned the difficulties of her situation.

"But it's all quite straightforward," Adalbert assured her for the hundredth time. "You're going to leave Gustl. We're going to have children . . ."

"Schnapps glasses, that's what I'll give birth to!" cried

Leopoldine. "It isn't straightforward at all, Bertl, none of it!"
She released herself and slid off the table. Some wood shavings
crackled beneath her shoes. When a customer threw up, the
proprietress would come along with a bucket of shavings and
obliterate the mess.

Leopoldine filled two glasses at the bar. Adalbert felt rather
depressed by her outburst, but he had long paid less heed to
what she said than to how she said it. When he and Leopoldine
were alone in the taproom, with candles flickering on the tables
and the counter, he was gripped by the peculiar sensation that
he himself was the navel of the world.

Leopoldine disappeared into the kitchen. He was about to
get off the table when she returned. His heart gave such a jump
that he momentarily feared for his life. Leopoldine was naked.
A variety of thoughts invaded his head: she wanted him to
possess her completely; she was play-acting; she had gone
mad.

She brought the two glasses of schnapps over to the table.
Adalbert didn't venture to ask what she had in mind. "Do I
have to take my clothes off too?" he asked, half in jest, half
embarrassed. He saw that she was holding a slip of paper in
which something seemed to be wrapped. Leopoldine unfolded
it to reveal a small quantity of white powder – about as much
as would cover the point of a knife. Taking a pinch between
thumb and forefinger, she dropped it into one of the glasses
and swirled it around, then did the same with the other.

"Poison?"

Poison!

There came a moment in every card game when Adalbert
resolved to take a chance. Thereafter he gave no more thought
to his decision and blindly put it into effect. Now, when their

eyes met, he realized it was all a joke: he would survive the potion. Leopoldine was putting him to the test.

He picked up his drink and clinked glasses with her. The mixture didn't taste too odd; she had probably put a little salt in it. After a lingering kiss, Adalbert sank back and folded his arms behind his head. Leopoldine lay down beside him.

"I want you to dream you can fly," she whispered. "You've never flown in a dream before, have you? Well, you're to fly in this one. All will be light and bright. You'll feel free as air and see the world from above. I'll be there too, flying ahead of you, behind you, beside you. We can hold hands and soar over churches and meadows. The sun is warm and balmy. Don't be afraid, just fly. We're all alone. Everything is so very, very far away. It's simple . . ."

"I'm flying. I can see a stretch of countryside with a solitary house in its midst. It's our house. Smoke is rising from the chimney. We have plenty of wood, so we won't be cold when we get back from our flight. Behind the house there's a stable."

"Can you see the sheep? A little girl is tending them – our daughter. It isn't wintertime, either, so we've no need for a fire. It's summertime. There are flowers blooming everywhere."

Adalbert kept his eyes shut. He felt as if he were spinning and falling at the same time, was afraid he might be sick. How tired he was! He clasped Leopoldine to him and inhaled the scent of her. The images he saw became more and more blurred. Leopoldine's voice seemed to rustle like leaves in the wind.

Carl's greatest fear after his illness was of war. In school he had heard of the emperor's battles with the Prussians and of the many men who had been killed in them. He trembled to think that someone might offend the emperor once more, in which case his father might have to go off and fight. Who could guarantee that he would ever come back? Officers, on the other hand, were sitting pretty in wartime. Very few of them were wounded or killed. The more they knew about war, the higher their rank. Men of that sort were duty-bound to lead the army from the rear. Being especially valuable in battle, they had to take shelter in well-protected positions.

Carl, who had expounded the advantages of being an officer to his father, asked why he didn't become one. "Me, an officer?" Adalbert laughed darkly. "I'm safe from going to war in any case. If they try to conscript me I'll shoot my foot off, and that'll be that! Who needs a cripple when charging the enemy?"

Carl didn't like to picture his father without a foot. And what about himself, if there was a war when he grew up? He would never bring himself to shoot his foot off, but he did not want to die, either. There was only one answer: he would have to become an officer. And, while waiting to be old enough, he would have to practise directing battles until his skill was such that the protection accorded him was second only to that enjoyed by the emperor!

But how should he practise making war? That decision came easy to him. Carl loved playing chess at school, and what was chess if not a war game? You led your own army against another. The object of the game was to checkmate your opponent's king, in other words, to defeat him. The other pieces – pawns, bishops, knights, rooks, and even the queen – served only to defend your king and attack your opponent's. They were worth nothing themselves, just like common soldiers in a real war. And Carl was the director of operations with the telescope.

He now focused all his ambitions on the game, which

enthralled him in itself, and not just because it held out the prospect of attaining general's rank. His father had taught him the rules, but they only played together one afternoon because Adalbert was spending less and less time at home. It wasn't until Carl changed schools that he found other boys to play with. To him, chess soon became more than a mere pastime. Although he took great pleasure in the game itself, what he enjoyed most of all was the feeling that possessed him at the end of a contest in which an opponent had failed to defeat him.

No one had a chess set at school, of course, and Carl was forbidden to take his father's board and pieces out of the house. He and his opponent – generally Franz – resorted to drawing a chess set on paper. When they moved a piece, they rubbed it out and redrew it in the appropriate square. Carl spent nearly all his time in class playing pencil chess. He was unable to muster any interest in the teacher's lessons. Before long, playing one opponent wasn't enough for him. Every player in the class with a piece of paper to hand had to pit himself against Carl, who would sometimes play seven or eight such games at once.

Carl liked Franz, to whom he owed the fact that the others no longer bullied him. Indeed, now that they occupied adjoining desks Carl's opinion carried more weight, when Franz was around, than that of many other boys in the class. He could not quite fathom why Franz should have chosen him as a friend. Although he felt sure Franz liked him, there was something about his friendship that made Carl recoil. Franz was nice on some occasions and nasty on others. But it wasn't his friend's erratic manner that disconcerted him. It was the very warmth of Franz's affection that confused and somehow touched him deeply. If the truth be told, this feeling probably had less to do with Franz than with Carl himself. Unable to cope with it, Carl felt impelled to decline all Franz's invitations to spend an afternoon playing chess at his home. Where the afternoons were concerned, he had to look for other opponents.

One frosty day in December, when Carl came home from school with his mother, his father had not yet left the house. Already dressed to go out, but looking unkempt and unshaven, he was blowing smoke rings across the breakfast table. Carl made his request.

"You'd like a game of chess, would you? By all means, but I'm afraid I don't have the time right now."

And he was out of the door in a trice.

Carl refused to be discouraged. His craving for chess inspired him with a daring idea. Having set up the chessboard beside the washbasin in his parents' room, he opened the game with his king's pawn and left a slip of paper alongside: "Your move, please. Thank you. Best regards, Carl." Maria grumbled that his father would never lend himself to such nonsense. If he didn't put the board away at once, she'd do so herself. But Carl dug his heels in. "It isn't in the way," he pleaded. "Let's leave it where it is. If Papa wants to play, fair enough; if not, I'll put it away, I promise."

Carl stared into the darkness for a long time that night, periodically pinching himself so as not to fall asleep and miss his father's homecoming. Awakened by his mother in the morning, he threw back the blankets and jumped out of bed with none of his usual complaints about the cold. He flung open the door so eagerly that it hit the wall with a crash. His father's snores were muffled by the bedclothes. Barefoot, Carl darted across the icy floor to the wash-stand. The move had been made! His father had also advanced his king's pawn two squares!

"He moved! He's playing me!" Carl exclaimed in a low voice. Without hesitating, he sent off his queen to set a trap for his father. Then he looked at the bed.

Adalbert was lying huddled up with only his thinning hair visible above the quilt. Carl was deeply affected by the sight. His father was playing him! There he lay, worn out with work, possibly drunk, possibly not. His poor, weary head, his poor hair!

Carl put out his hand, only to withdraw it when he noticed the look on his mother's face. He waited for her to turn away, vaguely ashamed of showing his emotions, then he stroked his father's head. He rubbed his eyes, unable to account for the turmoil within him.

So that was how Carl and Adalbert played chess. Adalbert did not fall into the trap. He would douse his head in the washbasin late at night and make his move. Carl no longer needed to be roused by Maria in the mornings. By the time she opened her eyes, he would already be at the wash-stand, studying the game. Neither he nor his father displayed great artistry at the board, and it was their very blunders that made the game drag on for weeks. This nocturnal game of chess – Adalbert had never countered Carl's latest move by lunchtime the following day – did not hold the same importance for both players. Adalbert smiled at Carl's obsession as one laughs at a dog that never tires of retrieving a stick. As for Carl, he was so engrossed in the state of the game that he went without sleep.

Although Carl was a pale, quiet, rather unapproachable boy, he wasn't predominantly joyless by nature. He could lie in the grass for hours, happily contemplating a tree. On the few occasions when Maria let him out, he would join some younger children in the street and play hide-and-seek or soldiers with them, sometimes forgetting his mother's injunction to be home before nightfall. In summer the feel of the ground beneath his bare feet lent him that inner poise which an eight- or twelve-year-old does not perceive as something transient but takes for granted. Being too weak to hold his own physically with children of the same age, however, he devoted his energies to developing his mind. He had nothing else to do, after all. Carl was not a melancholy boy; he simply did more thinking than others of his age.

The youngest of the children with whom Carl used to play in the street was Robert, a tough, tousled little boy with a nose that ran like a tap. Whenever there was dangerous terrain to be reconnoitred, Robert was despatched to check it out. His function was to run minor errands or beg money from his mother to buy sweets for the others. If a prank was to be played at some risk to the person who played it, the choice would fall on Robert. The rest looked on and laughed at a safe distance as he unhitched the horses from a cab and shooed them away or was lashed by a vigilant cabby's whip. Robert quite enjoyed this role. His temerity often made him the centre of attention, even though this tended to be a dubious pleasure. He could hardly be excluded from amusements of a more agreeable nature, however, because there was always a chance he might be needed.

One summer afternoon, Carl and the others had been lying idly in a field, at a loss for something to do. Out of sheer boredom, someone hit on the idea of goading Robert into performing some exceptional feat. "Bet you wouldn't dare to . . ." worked on him like a charm. "Bet you would dare to cut Frau X's washing line! Bet you wouldn't venture into that vicious watchdog's kennel!"

Robert passed all his tests of courage without demur. He wept with rage when accused, again and again, of being too scared to do this or that. The others roared with laughter at his defiant alacrity. Their suggestions became steadily sillier. Robert was prevailed on to eat some desiccated earthworms and roll a dog turd into balls.

They debated Robert's next task. Carl, who had been watching these goings-on with a detachment proper to the eldest of the party, went over to a tree to relieve himself. All at once, Robert appeared beside him. The little boy regarded him with a scowl. "Like to bet I wouldn't put your thing in my mouth?" he said.

Carl was dumbfounded. One of the youngsters yelped with delight. Robert stood with legs astraddle on the tree's protuberant roots, one hand resting on his hip, the other wiping the snot from his nose.

"You wouldn't dare," said Carl.

Robert bent down . . .

The others' laughter was incredulous, almost embarrassed. Carl gave a downward glance, then stepped back abruptly and buttoned his flies. Robert jumped up and punched the air with a triumphant yell. Carl felt so ashamed, he never wanted to set eyes on any of the boys again. He made some excuse and hurried home.

Carl never felt like joining the others in the street after that. Unwilling to be reminded of that awful business under the tree, he dismissed it from his mind. His one remaining fear was of bumping into one of the boys by chance, so he avoided their haunts.

He was doubly glad, therefore, to have discovered chess at his new school. Once he had started the game with his father, he lost any urge to go out and play. He lingered at the wash-stand every afternoon, studying the board or dreaming of his future as a general in the Austro-Hungarian army. His mother's objections were shyly but firmly brushed aside. "But I must play," he told her, "or I'll never learn." When asked why in the world he wanted to learn such a useless game, he did not reply.

It was not the thought of war alone that filled Carl with dread. He had an ambivalent attitude towards the night. Without being able to explain why, he felt convinced that the night was a living thing. There were times when his fear of the dark was such that he could only go to sleep sitting up in bed. He sensed the proximity of ghosts, the most terrible of which was the woman from the procession, who pursued him with her ripped and gaping belly. Then again, there were nights when fatigue overcame him because he felt so snug beneath the bedclothes. On those occasions he conceived of the night as a thinking, sentient being that conversed with and cared for him. The night was a capricious mother in whose arms he dwelt when day was done.

Lechner, who looked in at the Gasthaus zum Hirschen from time to time to see how Adalbert was faring, was one of the few people whose company the fiddler welcomed. Lechner knew of his love for Leopoldine. Adalbert was gnawed by a growing desire to confide in people, even virtual strangers, and allude to the turmoil that had been transforming his life in recent weeks. To Lechner, whom he trusted, he could speak of Leopoldine without restraint. He could communicate his thoughts, which forever revolved, not only around Leopoldine, but, more particularly, around the man who stood in the way of his happiness. He discussed his campaign against Gustl with Lechner, who forbore to offer advice or remind him of his responsibilities toward Maria and Carl. Adalbert was grateful for this. To him, Lechner's good-humoured countenance seemed to augur the fulfilment of his hopes.

Adalbert was more than usually glad of Lechner's company one night. A regular customer, who had just entered the taproom, whispered to him that Maria was outside. Furiously, Adalbert stubbed out his cigarette and joined her. Maria's face was a pale blob in the darkness.

"What is it? Is it Carl?"

"Liesl's with him," she said. "Come home."

He looked at her. Her eyes, which he seemed to have known forever, returned his gaze like those of some wrathful deity. His mood mellowed from one moment to the next. He felt compassionate.

"Why not come inside?" he said. "Have something to eat – I'll get them to put it on the slate. That's right, come along . . ." He took her by the shoulder, opened the door, and towed her after him. "I'm sure you haven't had a hot meal today."

He led her over to a table. "I haven't eaten at all," she murmured, as he sat her down on a chair.

"It's ages since we went out together," he said. "What about Carl – has he had a square meal today?"

"Don't worry, Carl can't complain." Adalbert made to get up and go, but she caught his arm.

He ordered two schnapps and a bowl of goulash for Maria. She refused the schnapps, so he clinked the glasses and drained them both. She made a grimace of distaste, which he ignored. For a while he tried to make conversation. He paid her some clumsy compliments, asked what needlework she had in hand, spoke of the sun, which hadn't shown itself for weeks, and told her about Lechner's new gloves. Finally, when he became aware that their conversation was verging on the nonsensical, he beckoned Lechner over and invited him to join them.

Lechner gave Maria one of his warmest smiles and called for a pitcher of red wine. He began by complimenting her on her appearance, then made her laugh by describing how he had bought his gloves. He held forth like a paid entertainer while Adalbert stared stiffly at the ceiling. When Maria had finished her goulash, Lechner suggested playing an innocuous card game for two. Having given Maria a perfunctory kiss, Adalbert excused himself and went over to the bar.

"What did you promise him in return?" asked the proprietress. She jerked her head at the table, where Lechner was playing cards with much boyish laughter.

"I'm a fool," Adalbert hissed. "Why didn't I send her home?" He half turned. Maria's looks repelled him.

He drank several glasses of schnapps. It was the time of night when the doorbell never stopped tinkling. His ear caught a particular note that had no connection with the bell itself. Without turning round, he knew that Leopoldine had just invested the room with her special magic. He ordered himself a treble.

When he woke up in bed the next day, neither Maria nor Carl was at home. The door and the windows were wide open, and he had no idea how he had got in. He remembered very little of the previous night. Leopoldine had come to the inn accompanied by Gustl. With evident amusement, Lechner and the proprietress sought opportunities to distract Maria's and Gustl's attention and grant Adalbert a few moments alone with Leopoldine. Adalbert picked a quarrel by neatly snubbing Gustl, who ended by kissing him and assuring him of his high regard. Maria, in a better mood, was escorted home by Lechner. Leopoldine drank one schnapps too many and felt very sick, so Gustl insisted on their leaving. For a while, Adalbert followed the couple like a demented ghost. Then, by a devious route, he tottered back to the inn, where the proprietress and Lechner, who had suddenly reappeared, were waiting. He knocked back several more schnapps and started to sob, reeling around the taproom. In the end he lay down on the shavings and passed out.

On the evening after that eventful night, Adalbert took out his fiddle and played it in one of the wine gardens where he was still welcome. Although completely out of practice, he soon got into his stride because he *wanted* to play. Not the cloying taproom melodies he detested so heartily, but classical music of a wild and passionate nature. He played as if possessed by the devil. No one in the establishment had ever heard the like.

The next day, with Carl's hand in his and the money he had earned in his pocket, he called on Samuel Gold, who ran a bookshop not far from the Gasthaus zum Hirschen. He put some coins on the counter and told the bookseller, without more ado, that the money was all he had. It would have to suffice to equip Carl with a chessboard, a set of chessmen to go with it, and the principal textbooks on playing the game. Adalbert said good-bye to Carl, shook hands with Gold, and assured him that the boy would be collected in two hours' time at the latest. Carl never saw his father again.

Adalbert went home to Maria and confessed his love for Leopoldine. Impatient of her despairing cries, he announced that he would be lodging with Lechner for the time being. That done, he proceeded to pack the barest essentials. At the door he asked his sobbing wife, who to him seemed no more than a figure in a dream, to collect Carl from Gold's bookshop. Going to the Gasthaus zum Hirschen, where Leopoldine was as usual serving behind the bar that Friday, he told her that he loved her and had left his wife. He would go to Lechner's to await the decision he now implored her to make, no matter how long it took or which way it went. Till then, he would leave her in peace.

Adalbert left the inn with his suitcase filled almost to the brim with bottles of schnapps. For two days he raved, bellowed and whimpered in his room, sang melancholy songs that few had sung before him, and led the Lechners to believe he was losing his reason. On the third night he broke out of his self-imposed cell and prowled around the Gasthaus zum Hirschen in the hope of seeing Leopoldine. Only native cunning enabled him to elude a constable who had taken exception to the bottle of spirits in his hand. On the fourth night he lurked outside the windows behind which he knew Maria and Carl to be asleep in bed. On the fifth night he staggered into the inn after closing time and slept with the proprietress. The next day he resolved to hang himself but could not summon up the courage. On the seventh night he could not stand it any longer. He hurried off to the inn to see Leopoldine. A whole week away from her was more than he could endure, he said. He expected her to betray regret, prevaricate, offer words of consolation, but no: to his joy and disbelief, he saw that her heart leapt when she looked at him.

Leopoldine was not only his prize but the arbiter of his campaign against Gustl. She now declared him the victor. Gustl came to the inn to embrace Adalbert and, with complete sincerity, to wish him all the best. Adalbert could not look him in the eye.

Maria was loath to let Adalbert go. When he called at the apartment to collect some clean shirts, she gave him a terrible reception. She clung to his knees, her expression such a mute cry of pain that it brought tears of pity to his eyes. In the end she handed him a little parcel. He found it to contain a pair of gloves and some thick stockings, together with bread, ham, bacon, and a few coins which she had contrived, by some impossible means, to set aside.

To occupy the tantalizing hours during which Leopoldine was obliged to work at the inn, she and Adalbert had discovered a new game: sensing the other's gaze and smiling at the thought of it. The rest of the time they spent in the Lechners' little guest room, where they told each other their life stories and often – to begin with, at least – drank themselves into a stupor.

One day, while they were strolling on the Kahlenberg, Adalbert came to a halt, spread his arms, and challenged Leopoldine to let herself fall; he would catch her, he said. She didn't hesitate for an instant. He caught her a hand's-breadth short of the ground.

Those were the happiest weeks of Adalbert's life. His heart ceased its strenuous work just when he had begun to refrain from drinking every day. Seven months after his death Leopoldine gave birth to a little girl. She herself died of influenza soon after Lina was born.

| 5 |

From Carl's point of view, his assignation with Anna Feiertanz could not have come at a worse time. They had arranged to meet at the Café Renaissance, and he would naturally have to pay the bill. His fee from the *Deutsche Schachzeitung* had covered his rent and a few modest meals, but where was he to find the ten-crown note the evening was bound to cost? He could hardly say, "I'm afraid you'll have to pay for your own coffee, dear lady."

Many coffee houses were haunted by wealthy chess enthusiasts eager to play a master for money. You gave them knight's odds, beat them notwithstanding, and pocketed the stake. For Carl, this was out of the question. He was too scrupulous to want to cheat anyone. Borrowing was another possibility, but even that wouldn't do. He could never bring himself to ask anyone for anything, so he had to discard the idea of soliciting an advance from one of the many chess periodicals he wrote for.

This problem nagged at Carl all day long. He tried to take his mind off it by analysing the opening systems Lasker had employed so far, but without success. It was almost as if he feared doing Frau Feiertanz an injury if he didn't pay for her coffee. He even considered sending someone to the café with a message to the effect that he was ill.

He ended by pawning the watch he'd won at the Carlsbad tournament three years before. Then, feeling relieved, he hurried back to his lodgings and immersed himself in Lasker's interpretation of the Ruy Lopez. When the time came he sneaked into the nearest coffee house and made straight for the lavatory, where he had a wash. It occurred to him on the way to the Café Renaissance that one presented a lady with flowers, but where to acquire some in winter? He went into a shop and bought a bunch of artificial roses. They were almost indistinguishable from the real thing, to his eye, though they had no scent.

He had been sitting over a coffee for quite some time when Anna came hurrying towards him. He rose awkwardly to his feet. "Please!" she exclaimed. "Don't get up." She flopped down on the banquette and gave him a cheerful wink. Her cheeks were glowing. Jumping up again, she slipped off her coat and draped it over the waiter's arm, then ordered herself a liqueur and a pastry. Her eye fell on the flowers, which she found appalling. The next moment she burst out laughing. She wondered if such tastelessness was typical of all chess players.

"So tell me," she said. "Why do you want to become world champion?"

"I don't quite understand . . ."

"As world champion you'd be famous. You wouldn't be forgotten . . ."

"I'm not sure that's what I want."

"But you're playing for the world championship. Why?"

Carl ran a hand over his hair.

"What about you?" he asked, scratching at a speck of food

on his trousers. "Why are *you* interested in the world championship? Could it be that you're planning to write a book about it?"

"Would you find that so strange? I've considered it, but I think I'm too imaginative."

She explained the apparent contradiction. By imagining herself doing this or that, she anticipated the event and rendered it unnecessary to put her intention into effect.

Carl wasn't sure he had understood her correctly. He asked her to explain her idea once more. Although he could not altogether associate himself with what she said, the longer he thought about it the more it appealed to him.

Anna's choice of conversational gambit was quite deliberate. She knew that Carl Haffner was extremely shy. She also knew, however, that the best way of changing people is to treat them as if they already were what you wish them to be. Anna not only talked to Carl as if his insecurity did not exist; she employed another device as well. In order to extract a secret from someone, you have to divulge one yourself. Although her disclosures to Carl were no secrets, she did reveal aspects of her character that would normally have been concealed from a person she knew only slightly. Without becoming overfamiliar, she chatted away as uninhibitedly as if they were old acquaintances.

After his second coffee, Carl was amazed at the things he was telling this woman. He let himself be talked into having a liqueur. To prevent it from going to his head, he ordered himself some rolls and a slice of cake. Anna told him about all the parties she went to. He slapped his thigh at her description of the strange types who disported themselves at these gatherings, and she made him promise to accompany her some time. He gave no more thought to the question that had preoccupied him, namely, what she wanted of him. Did any woman really take it into her head to accost a person on the strength of a newspaper article, simply to make his acquaintance?

After a second liqueur Carl forgot about the world championship and Lasker. He felt good. It was only when Anna suddenly addressed him by his first name that she reduced him to embarrassment once more.

Carl signalled for the bill. He reached for his wallet, took out a banknote, and proffered it to the waiter. When he looked up, Anna was putting some change in her bag. The waiter bowed. The note was still in Carl's hand. He opened his mouth, but no sound emerged.

"You can pay next time."

They said good-bye outside the café. Anna wished him luck for tomorrow's game. He was so flummoxed, he forgot to offer to see her home.

For the fourth game, play was transferred to the Café Marienbrücke. Hummel's regular haunt could accommodate many more spectators than the Vienna Chess Club. Mandl had taken it into his head to make capital out of the championship, so the separate room was summarily done away with. The table was set up in the middle of the café, and anyone wishing to watch the game had to pay an entrance fee.

Before the game, a simultaneous display took place. The organizers had devised a special entertainment: Lasker and Haffner were to play twenty opponents, making alternate moves without mutual consultation. Lasker, who breezed into the café ten minutes before play was due to start, nodded his acknowledgement of the applause that surged to meet him on all sides. He threaded his way through the onlookers, as erect and light on his feet as ever. Mandl came bustling up. Lasker drew him firmly aside.

"I noticed your cashier at the entrance. Have they all paid to get in?" Lasker indicated the massed spectators. Just then they started to applaud again, even more enthusiastically than before. Haffner had forced his way into the café at Fähndrich's heels.

Mandl mumbled a halting explanation, but Lasker cut him short. "Save your breath, Herr President. You forget who has brought these people here. Thirty per cent of the entrance money for Haffner and me, and the proceedings can begin. Thirty per cent, or I refuse to play and cancel the whole contest."

Lasker turned and sauntered calmly over to Carl to bid him good day and explain what had happened. Carl ventured no opinion on the matter. Although he was reluctant to offend Lasker, he had no wish to associate himself with such an unpleasant request. Meanwhile, Mandl had hurried over to Rothschild. He meekly conveyed the news, but could not forbear to add that he considered the world champion distastefully avaricious. Rothschild did not deign to reply. He found Lasker standing outside the café, extended a suave apology, and affirmed that the world champion's request was perfectly right and proper. The money would be paid as soon as it had been counted. The whole thing was simply due to lack of communication between the organizers.

"You see?" Lasker said with a smile. "I thought as much." Having told Carl, he went and stood in readiness beside the twenty chessboards. Mandl delivered his address of welcome in a chilly voice.

Lasker was the first to pass along the rows. Carl shook hands with each opponent and made the second move. When he bent over the last board, he could not believe his eyes. He blushed. "You never told me you played chess."

"I shall need help," Anna replied with a grin. She gestured behind her. Every board had its cluster of spectators, but her own was positively besieged.

Lasker had devised a plan for this simultaneous display. What could be more logical than to use these games as a rehearsal for the contest ahead – to strengthen himself and ruffle Haffner's composure a trifle? They jointly commanded the white pieces on every board, so Lasker was able, for once, to influence Haffner's own position directly. He proceeded to place all twenty boards in such a precarious position that the masters on watch outside the café brayed with laughter. Not even the boldest Romantics among them would have dreamt of mounting so reckless an attack. Carl was in no mood to laugh. He felt terribly uncomfortable in Lasker's preordained positions. The world champion was burning all their bridges behind them. Given the said positions, switching to a defensive, more temperate game would have led straight to disaster. Carl was obliged to join in these daredevil, wholly unmotivated onslaughts and pray that he was up against weak opponents. Lasker had calculated correctly: his unwonted style of play was sapping Carl's energy.

Carl spent a long time deep in thought at Anna's board. It would be gentlemanly not to defeat her, he felt, but he could not make it too obvious. However, he was so flustered by Lasker's bizarre tactics, and so embarrassed by their previous evening's encounter, that he made some really maladroit moves at her board. He played so badly, in fact, that

Lasker wagged his finger at him as they were changing over. "What's the matter with you, Haffner?" he demanded. "Are you in love?"

Anna had some eager assistants, of course. After each of the masters' moves, she was showered from all quarters with whispered advice on the best response. Donning her most cordial smile, she asked one of her admirers, who had been devoting himself to her game with excessive zeal, if he would care to change places with her. He failed to take the hint. "No, no, madame," he tittered. "It's your game, madame. You're playing wonderfully well."

Anna waved to some friends who had come at her invitation and were following the proceedings with interest. She was occupying her chair only because she wanted to observe the spectacle from that particular angle. The game itself didn't matter to her.

Carl's poor play granted her an early victory. The café rang with applause. Anna brushed the congratulations aside and thanked the circle of whisperers behind her board. Ties were straightened, moustaches twirled, and the sunniest smiles displayed. The gentlemen lamented the fact that Anna had to attend to her friends once more.

So the game against the only lady in the field was past redemption. Carl managed not to lose another. He did not play his strongest chess by any means – he found the positions too awkward and unfamiliar for that – but at least he did not ruin matters for Lasker, who felt at home in such bizarre positions. Suddenly, it was three to one in favour of the masters: checkmate on Board 7, checkmate on Board 15, resignation on Board 4. There followed two more resignations on Boards 3 and 6 and checkmate on Board 12.

Lasker conceded only one draw, and that was attributable to an error by Carl, who had run out of time because of a needless defensive move. The final result was eighteen to one. It was a perfect demonstration of Lasker's resolve, courage, and strength. Carl had been relegated to a supernumerary role, and he sensed it. Hummel and the Viennese masters puffed at their cigars, looking abashed. They were no novices, the people Lasker had defeated. Apart from the charming lady on Board 20, all were unknown but strong players from the furthest corners of the empire.

The course of this demonstration match mirrored the successes Lasker had scored in serious games for the past twenty years. He could be down and out after a few moves and win regardless. Many people accused him of being downright lucky, but luck, of course, had no bearing on his victories. Lasker accepted losses in order to lure an opponent on to dangerous ground. He counted on being the stronger at the crucial moment. A foolhardy system of this kind would have spelled disaster to any other player, but not to Lasker. He *was* the stronger – and not just at the crucial moment. Many of his moves seemed to smack of insanity. Very few people grasped the well-founded and carefully calculated nature of his play. "This move is fine against Tarrasch; against Janowski it would be a gross error," he once said while analysing a game. His listeners thought he was joking, but he wasn't. Lasker tailored his play to an opponent's character. Many people felt bewitched by the world champion, many believed he had hypnotic powers. There was hardly a player in the world who understood Lasker's philosophy.

Why was Carl Haffner proof against this method? Carl himself did not know how he had already held Lasker to a draw three times, but Lasker knew the reason: the Viennese master refused to take his bait. Whatever Lasker did, and whatever outrageously inviting manœuvres he employed, Carl remained in his burrow. He flatly refused to accompany his opponent to the brink of the precipice where, for Lasker, the real battle began.

Hummel paced to and fro, plucking at his hair, while Carl and Lasker were sitting down to their fourth game. If Carl had been shaken by the world champion's stratagem, he feared the worst. One had only to read their expressions. Lasker was sitting more erect than ever. Carl's face looked as if he had dusted it with flour – and he, Hummel, was to blame. The simultaneous match had been his suggestion. Even a brandy failed to steady Hummel's nerves. He did not calm down until, after a good hour, Carl rose and started talking to Frau Feiertanz.

Anna introduced her companions. Carl, who instantly forgot their names, asked her for a brief word in private. Leading her over to a secluded corner, he pulled out his wallet.

Anna waved it away. "Certainly not. I told you: you can pay next time."

"Please," he insisted. "Take it . . . take the money. How can I possibly . . ."

"Quite so! How can you possibly worry about it?" She caught hold of his arm. "Now tell me, what in heaven's name is the problem?"

Carl stared at her, then retracted his head like a tortoise and went back to the board. Anna introduced her friends to the president and commended his helpfulness. Mandl, who had been slinking disconsolately across the room, blossomed at once.

Hummel had underestimated Carl's resilience. Lasker marvelled yet again at the extent of the transformation he underwent when seated at the board. All at once, his hesitation and uncertainty vanished. Although Lasker succeeded in gaining an advantage, Carl put up such a stubborn, circumspect and faultless defence that his position was impenetrable.

Hummel was overjoyed when the game ended in an armistice. Scenting new recruits to his Anti-Duel League, he had button-holed Anna's friends. Carl went over to her and produced the banknote again. She looked him in the eye, and even a blind man would have seen that she really didn't know what he expected of her.

She smiled. "I'll take the money, but on one condition: that we meet again in the next few days. I'll choose the time and place, and I'll foot the bill."

Carl gave in. He was so glad to have paid off his embarrassing debt that he agreed to Anna's proposal without hesitation. He wouldn't eat or drink a thing on the evening in question, he told himself. He might even manage to talk her into letting him do the gentlemanly thing again.

The fifth game was the last to take place on Viennese soil. After a four-day break the contest was to move to Berlin, where the remaining games would be played.

Hummel, previewing the fifth game in his chess column, pulled out all the stops once more. Journalists converged from all over Europe, and the windows of the Café Marien-brücke got broken in the resulting mêlée. Neither of the opponents could force an entry, so the game had to be post-poned for half an hour.

Lasker finally stumbled into the café, looking rather bruised and battered. "Would I were a Viennese," he said with a chuckle, every inch the cosmopolitan. Only the arbiter beside him heard this remark, which was drowned by the din.

Carl reached the entrance with the help of Fähndrich, who had developed into something of a pugilist in recent weeks. Once inside the café, Carl fainted. His face was deathly pale, his forehead beaded with sweat. A doctor came forward at once. Carl was carried over to a bench, where the physician felt his pulse, called for a glass of water, and administered smelling salts. The fainting fit, he surmised, had been brought on by having to forge a path through the crush. He wasn't to know that Carl had eaten nothing for days apart from the rolls and the slice of cake he'd consumed on his night out with Anna. He was utterly destitute, having thought it inappropriate to accept his share of the fee for the simultaneous match.

Carl opened his eyes. When asked by the arbiter if he wished to postpone the game, he merely requested a half-hour's delay. Did he feel up to playing such an exacting game? One could not disappoint the spectators, he replied. Besides, he didn't want to be a nuisance to his opponent. The arbiter shrugged his shoulders. Hummel demanded to know if Carl was in his right mind, and Fähndrich implored him to defer the game. "I'll be all right, gentlemen," said Carl, brushing their entreaties aside.

Lasker wondered if he was up against a lunatic when Carl sat down at the board. This wasn't a club championship, after all. Or did the Viennese want to play the martyr? Lasker was on the point of lodging a protest. If he won this game, people would be able to insinuate that he had defeated a sick man.

No one was surprised, in fact, when Carl manœuvred himself into a poor position. He didn't once get up and leave the board, and nearly every master on the premises predicted his defeat.

The world champion was palpably in the ascendant when, at Fähndrich's request, the arbiter adjourned the game for three days to enable Carl to recuperate.

Fähndrich and the Viennese masters conveyed Carl to the chess club in Rothschild's automobile. He protested, but to no avail. Almost under duress, they put him to bed in the rest room, where the doctor gave him a roborant injection. Fähndrich watched over him from a chair beside the bed. When Carl had gone to sleep, Weiss took Fähndrich's place. Also among his supervisors were Mandl and Rothschild himself, each of whom spent an hour sitting at his bedside. Once he had slept his fill, they ordered a meal from a restaurant. Carl refused to eat it. Fähndrich threatened to spoon the food into his mouth, and Hummel backed him up with some ripe expletives. Carl had perforce to comply. He was just as unsuccessful in opposing their insistence on keeping him a prisoner at the chess club until the game was resumed.

Every pretext failed. He said he needed to change his clothes; to his mortification, Rothschild kitted him out with new ones from head to foot. He said he had to go home at once to write an article; Hummel enquired the subject of the article and wrote it for him. As a last resort, Carl feigned an urgent desire to see his mother, who might, he said, be in need of his help. Maria was astonished to receive a visit from the three leading lights of the Vienna Chess Club, who presented her with a box of chocolates and offered to assist her in any and every way.

Carl was allowed out only for a daily walk, and then it was under the supervision of four chess enthusiasts. He received two visits a day from the doctor and was made to eat breakfast, lunch and dinner. When the three days were up, the Viennese chess masters agreed that they had never seen their champion in finer fettle. Carl was driven back to the Café Marienbrücke by car. In an agony of embarrassment, he swore to himself that he would repay every crown that had been spent on him as soon as possible.

Carl sat down at the board refreshed. He could not afford to lose this game – this game above all. He was in his colleagues' debt. They expected him to hold his own.

His position was genuinely poor. He almost buried his head in the board, sickened by the thought of Hummel's melancholy expression. He had never played so doggedly before, but in vain; Lasker soon had him at a disadvantage. On the face of it, the world champion was bound to go into the lead after this game. Except that – as Lasker himself used to say – nothing is harder to win than a game already won.

Carl abandoned all his inhibitions. He sacrificed a pawn and launched a counter-attack – his only hope. Neutral observers rubbed their hands. The game was taking on some interest at last – it was no holds barred from now on – but the outcome seemed clear: Lasker ought to win. What did Monsieur Hummel think?

Hummel was staring at the board like someone who knows that a bomb is about to explode with ineluctable violence. He did not utter a word. The masters had long since deserted the demonstration boards outside the café. Albin and his associates were clustered around the table, craning their necks and shuffling from foot to foot.

The world champion began to run out of time. Disconcerted that Carl had counter-attacked with such ferocity, he made a precipitate move. Carl responded at once. Nothing could be heard but the click of the lever with which each player started his opponent's clock after a move. Lasker manœuvred with his queen. Carl sent his own queen deep into Lasker's position. Lasker hesitated. With bated breath, Hummel worked out a number of variations. The world champion had made a grave mistake, he realized, and Carl's foray with the queen had brought it to light. He had made an incredible, wonderful move.

Lasker shuffled around on his chair. He raised his arm as though to make a move, ran his fingers through his hair, then let his arm fall. Carl's face was glowing. Hummel worked out some more variations. Did Lasker have any form of defence left? None that Hummel could see. The significance of this development flashed through his mind. For a fraction of a second, he almost went insane.

Lasker withdrew his rook. Carl gave check with his rook and captured a pawn with his next move. Lasker summoned his queen to the rescue. Another two moves with his own queen, and Carl had sprung his trap. For several minutes, Lasker stared at the board without moving. Then he overturned his king and stopped the clock.

Hummel shouted until his throat hurt. No one stirred. Hummel continued to shout without realizing it. Then a figure dashed past him and hurled itself at Carl: Fähndrich. He bore Carl to the ground and hugged him. Weiss, Wolf and Albin hurled themselves on top of the pair. This spectacle jolted the onlookers out of their stupor. No one who witnessed the ensuing scenes of jubilation would ever forget them. Taciturn old Julius Thirring, who wanted Carl to win the world championship more fervently than anyone, stood in a corner, fighting back his tears. Hummel sprayed the throng with champagne. Lasker stole off unnoticed.

Midway through the world championship, the challenger was leading one-nil. To many people, this was an almost inconceivable sensation. Lasker had never before been behind in any match. And now, the man who was widely regarded as quasi-superhuman at the chessboard was losing to – of all people – the diffident little Viennese master. If Haffner were to draw the remaining five games or win as many of them as Lasker, he would be the new world champion.

Hummel's next headline read:

THE SUN HAS FALLEN FROM THE SKY.

At the celebration that set the seal on the Vienna section of the world championship, Carl was presented with an advance on his share of the purse. He took it over to Rothschild, intending to settle his debts, but Rothschild gave him such a look that he pocketed it again without a word. He had no better luck with Mandl. The president told him not to worry; all expenses were being borne by the club. Carl protested that the club was financed by private patrons. Why should those idealists pay for his meals?

Mandl cast his eyes up to heaven. Taking Carl by the arm, he propelled him in the direction of Anna, who was coming towards them with a champagne glass in each hand. "A woman'll cure him of his stupid ideas," he muttered at Carl's departing figure.

Anna extended her congratulations. She regretted having failed to elbow her way through the crowd and watch the game, she said, but she insisted on drinking a toast to his victory. Before they were separated, she reminded him of his promise and asked him to meet her at a café the following night. Carl said yes to everything. He forgot about his debts, drank some champagne, and suffered himself to be dragged through the establishment by ardent admirers. If only for a brief while, victory had awakened the effervescent side of his nature. For an hour or two he was a different person – one who could talk to people without feeling that they were sitting in judgement on him.

He spent the day before he left for Berlin relaxing at Lina's. After they had had a snack lunch together, she sat down at the piano. Still entranced by his victory over Lasker, Carl allowed his thoughts to wander. They turned to Anna. He didn't find the sight of her as unsettling as he had at first. Anna was a strange woman. He found her impossible to classify properly. She was so free and easy, so bold and unconstrained – too bold, perhaps. He admired her candid way of dealing with people. He envied her self-assurance in the street, in conversation, with head waiters. But it wasn't simply that she reminded him of his yearning for more self-assurance; confronted by her vivacity, he hankered to fall in love. It was many years since he had last given any thought to that desire. Not that he was in love with Anna. He didn't know why, but he felt nothing for any woman, apart from the one who was playing his favourite tune at that moment.

The wall clock struck. He looked up.

"Lina?"

No reply.

"Is anything the matter, Lina?"

She had stopped playing and was staring at the keyboard. Carl knew this of old. Sometimes, in the very middle of a conversation, Lina would look blank and fall silent, staring into space for twenty or thirty minutes. She could never say where she had been. "You've been dreaming, Lina," Carl would tell her. And she would look at him with eyes that had just been contemplating another world, and say "Would you care for some tea?" or something of the kind.

There was a knock at the door. Lina still didn't move. More knocking. Carl answered the door. It was one of Lina's piano pupils. He ushered her inside. The girl tiptoed shyly over to the piano and curtsied. Lina didn't look up. Carl put a finger to his lips and signalled to the girl to wait. He poured some tea and they sat down, avoiding each other's eye. Eventually, Lina stretched and rubbed her eyes. "Oh, you're here aleady," she said affably. The girl jumped up and gave a another bob. "Good afternoon, Frau Bauer."

Lina saw Carl out and wished him a successful trip. "Come back hale and hearty, world champion or not." They exchanged a hug. Carl left the house with a vague sense of deprivation.

His mother, who had swapped shifts with a colleague especially for the occasion, greeted him with a brimming plate. Carl pulled a face, but he ate up rather than make a scene. Maria also provided him with a parcel of clean linen and some useful tips for the journey. She warned him against draughts, told him to beware of Berlin cooking, and advised him on the safest place to hide his money. She said the same thing before every foreign tournament. Carl thanked her for everything. When she wasn't looking he slipped some of his purse money under the tablecloth. He had a horrific vision of the public lavatory where she worked.

Anna having left her flowers behind the café, Carl presumed that his choice of gift had been unsuitable. This time he bought her some chocolates. One could not go wrong with those.

A reporter appeared at his door. Although Carl was ashamed of his shabby lodgings, he had to invite the man in and answer his questions. Yes, he was looking forward to the championship; no, he didn't feel confident of winning. No, he had no political opinions. God save the emperor. He spent the time that remained until nightfall sweating over Lasker's opening system.

Anna turned up with several friends, two of whom Carl had already met. He ordered a glass of water, but Anna intervened. "Bring the gentleman . . ." She proceeded to enumerate a variety of drinks and sweet things which, in combination, would have turned any gourmet pale. Anna laughed. "Don't look so appalled," she said. "You don't have to eat the lot. Try them, at least." The others were just as liberal with their orders. Carl didn't dare object.

He stared at his fingernails, at the glowing tip of his cigar. Before long he could have drawn the interior of the café from memory. Anna spoke with him no more often, and no differently, than she did with the rest of the table. Her friends expressed an interest in him, asked him candid questions about his life, chatted together, discreetly drew him into conversation. He surveyed their faces. If only it hadn't been for all those slices of gâteau and liqueurs! They were positively foaming at the mouth.

When the waiter had stopped bringing delicacies to the table, Anna invited her friends to help themselves to the chocolates Carl had brought her. This annoyed him. He had purchased the chocolates for her, not for them.

After a final round of pear brandy, one friend after another took his leave. Carl remained behind with Anna. He longed to leave too, but that would have been discourteous. He tried not to think of the bill, did some mental arithmetic, and quailed. He did not even have enough money on him to pay for his own share.

"I've some news for you," said Anna. "We shall be seeing each other in Berlin as well. Herr Hummel can't go because he's too busy here with his newspaper articles. He has appointed me his correspondent."

"You? But you don't . . ."

"I don't know the first thing about chess? You're right, of course, but I've already mastered the notation. I have to telegraph the moves to Hummel after every game. That and a description of the atmosphere – that's what he wants. Does that sound so difficult?"

Anna wasn't as talkative this time as on their last assignation. She kept watching the people in the café, to which she was clearly no stranger. The piano player had greeted her very warmly. One or two of the tables were occupied by unescorted women. Anna ordered herself some wine. From time to time she glanced at Carl or drew his attention to a fellow customer.

Carl tried to imagine how Lina would feel in such an establishment. He had never gone out with her in the evening. Strictly speaking, their relations were limited to the visits he paid her at home. Was it proper for a woman and her brother to patronize a café at night, like a courting couple? What *could* a brother and sister do without offending against propriety?

Carl wondered if it was Anna's presence that made him brood like this. He studied her in profile. She was so engrossed in the other customers' facial expressions, it might have been a job of work. What was she looking for? She seemed relaxed, for all that, as if she were engaged in some activity that meant a great deal to her.

When the bill came, Carl didn't find it too hard to let Anna pay it. He offered to escort her home. She thanked him, but said she still had things to do. After all, she pointed out, they'd be seeing each other tomorrow in the train.

6

Maria gave up collecting Carl from school after Adalbert's death. He used to tiptoe back into the apartment at lunchtime, kiss his mother, and sit down at table. He didn't say a thing until the meal was over, and his first words were always the same: could he go and see Samuel Gold? Maria raised no objection. Carl gave her a hug, and she watched him run a comb through his hair before disappearing into his room, to emerge a moment later, notebook in hand, and hurry out of the apartment.

Maria was sometimes perturbed by her failure to curb Carl's activities and supervise his homework – by the fact that there was no man in the house to set him an example. What perturbed her even more, however, was the thought of hurting his feelings. No one could tell what was going on inside the boy. He hadn't wept when Adalbert died – not in her presence, at least – and the only wish he ever expressed was to visit Samuel Gold. On Sundays he stayed home and said nothing. His private thoughts were a mystery to everyone. Chess was his sole obsession, and Maria had no wish to deprive him of it.

At the back of Gold's bookshop was a small, low-ceilinged room which, to Carl, seemed the most congenial place on earth.

It was always in a state of cosy chaos. Books were stacked on the shelves, on the floor, on the table. Open newspapers were dusted with cigar ash, unwashed coffee cups lurked everywhere. The armchair was piled high with washing, cooking utensils, newspapers, and all manner of oddments such as notepads, toothbrushes, rheumatism cures, and carnival masks. It was easy to bump into things, and one was bound to become entangled in a fly-paper several times a day. Smoking in one corner was the leaky stove on which Gold brewed tea and coffee. The premises were so damp that he had to keep stoking it nearly all year round.

There was just room on the table for a chessboard, and this was where Carl received his tuition. Gold introduced him to the theories of Wilhelm Steinitz, the former world chess champion. He instructed Carl in opening systems, tutored him in strategy and tactics. Now and then, at Carl's insistence, they played a serious game. If the shop bell rang, Gold would clear the board, open a book of chess problems, and pick out a suitable one for Carl to solve. Having found it, he arranged the board accordingly and told the boy what he had to work out – checkmate in three, for example, or a surprise move that would guarantee a draw. Only then would he go and attend to his waiting customer.

Samuel Gold loved chess as a man can love poetry or painting without being a poet or painter himself. His greatest pleasure consisted in pure contemplation. Playing an opponent held no appeal for him. To Gold, chess was an almost unexplored land of infinite wealth. In his opinion, actually playing chess was a bar to making new discoveries on more important terrain. Although he was thinking primarily of chess problems, they were not his only concern. Attracted by the history of the game and its culture, he had built up the finest specialized library in Vienna. He was also a respected journalist who compiled the chess page of the *Allgemeine Sportzeitung* and was a freelance contributor to more than ten other publications.

Gold knew of Adalbert Haffner's death, of course, but had no precise knowledge of the attendant circumstances. Carl's mother, who came to the bookshop occasionally, would bring them both a snack and ask if the boy was being a nuisance. Gold replied, quite truthfully, that he found Carl's company most agreeable. It delighted him, not only to nurture Carl's talent, which he had spotted at once, but to expand his knowledge of the game and watch his understanding of it grow. He felt convinced that he was guiding the first steps of a future grandmaster. Even in the mornings he looked forward to the moment when the boy would rap on the shutter after school. Carl was an undemanding, taciturn companion. Whatever problem he was set, he would gaze avidly, with burning ears, at the chessboard. He also dispelled the loneliness that tended to weigh on Samuel Gold despite the pleasure he derived from the game.

In that smoky room at the back of Gold's bookshop, near a small park and a church whose bells sometimes intruded on an analysis, Carl engrossed himself in the world of feints, theoretical draw positions, and lost endgames. He thought of nothing but chess. In class he played his classmates with pencil and paper. He had long ago swept them aside with ease. Before they would consent to play him, they demanded that he eliminate his queen, or at least a rook, without compensation. It was so hard for him these days to find opponents, he had to dispel his boredom in class by reading books on chess. The teachers punished him, but he remained unmoved. He and they breathed the same air, but that was all.

Carl's conception of time was that of a Methuselah. He knew chess masters who had been dead for decades not merely by name; he was versed in their openings, their ideas, their style of play, and he also knew what they looked like, how they walked, and how and where they had lived. He could effortlessly summon up the smell of the room in which the London tournament of 1851 had taken place. He saw nothing odd in the fact that he sometimes conversed with François Philidor, the French chess master whose remains had been mouldering in the ground for almost a century. For him, anything to do with chess existed in the present, and the teachers who bawled and hauled him out in front of the class were merely figures in a dream from which he gradually awakened on the way home from school.

Carl neglected his lessons without evil intent. He was never impolite, far less impertinent. Later on, when asked if he had had to repeat a year at school, he could not answer because he simply did not know. But held back he was, two years in succession.

What he failed to learn soon enough was that boys who did poorly at school were precluded from an officer's career. But the army had ceased to attract him in any case. Banal ideas like those associated with warfare and the emperor no longer entered his mind. There was room in it for chess alone. To Carl, chess was a condition and Gold's back room a paradise on earth. He had no fixed aim, no desire other than to remain in the said condition. When he had been kept back a second year, however, his mother felt it was time to do something.

Terrible though it was that Adalbert had run off with another woman, Maria could have coped with that. He might come back, after all, and she was prepared to wait for ever. When she looked up at the morning sky, she consoled herself with the thought that Adalbert was doing the same, and that their lines of sight were intersecting at some point. It was good that they could both see the sun at the same moment. She derived strength from that idea. Then he was laid to rest in a pauper's grave, and the sun was hers alone to see.

Liesl moved in with Maria for the first few weeks after Adalbert's death. Lechner, too, was a frequent visitor. He went shopping, helped with the heavy work, and left money on the table. Despite her concern for Carl, Maria would never have managed without the pair of them. Lechner took Carl for walks, giving her an opportunity to weep without restraint in Liesl's arms. In the evenings she got drunk. Liesl and Lechner, who could see no harm in it, drank with her. There were situations in which alcohol was the surest prop and stay – provided one didn't remain dependent on it for too long.

While all manner of emotional scenes unfolded in the living-room, Carl pored over chess manuals in his bedroom. Lechner wondered what was going on inside the boy, and how much he absorbed of what went on around him. He didn't even glance up from his book when Lechner brought him some tea or bread. If addressed, he would raise his head after a while, his eyes so fixed and glassy that Lechner suspected he was feverish or smitten with insanity. Then, quite suddenly, his face cleared, and he would smile and say thank you. Lechner shrugged.

Liesl moved back into her own home, but she continued to visit Maria almost daily. Maria drained a bottle only two or three times a month now, usually when either Liesl or Lechner was keeping her company. On those occasions she sometimes lost her composure and would suddenly burst into tears, sobbing and wailing and tearing her hair. One night,

Lechner had had enough. He laid two fingers on her brow.

"It's over now," he said solemnly. "You've no need to cry any more. It's over. Everything's all right." Then he muttered something and pressed his fingers hard against Maria's forehead.

Liesl doubted whether this strange form of words had penetrated Maria's consciousness. They had all teased Lechner often enough about his penchant for witchcraft. He cultivated a reputation for possessing magical powers, or at least for being proficient in various esoteric branches of knowledge. Impressionable young people were happy to believe in Lechner's powers, especially when maudlin drunk. Not so Liesl, who regarded him as a lovable crackpot. When it occurred to her, months later, that she hadn't seen Maria crying lately, she dismissed this as a coincidence. For safety's sake, however, she included Lechner in her nightly prayers.

Maria became Vienna's youngest lavatory attendant. After traipsing from one government department to another in the hope of obtaining a widow's pension, she had been assigned a job in a public convenience. She could not imagine a more repugnant occupation, but at least she was no longer obliged to set off every few days to beg for more needlework. It had riled her for years to have to go down on her knees and thank people for the privilege of working her hands to the bone in return for a pittance.

Maria soon got over her distaste at having to work in a lavatory, but she took longer to become accustomed to something else. Her fellow lavatory attendants were toothless whores debarred from following their trade by the march of time. Maria now saw herself placed on a par with these coarse, worn-out women. If the ageing prostitutes rejected her, the men emerging from the cubicles brazenly propositioned her. She learned to cope with both categories. Being the youngest and prettiest woman present, she got the most tips. By suggesting that all gratuities be pooled and shared out equally, she won the prostitutes over.

It was harder to convince men that she did not pursue her colleagues' former profession. In the end, she gave up. The whores looked askance at her efforts to dissociate herself from them and the men refused to believe her, so she turned the tables on them. She either made assignations which she never kept, or, depending on her mood of the moment, sent the lechers packing with a volley of crude oaths. She soon mastered the requisite vocabulary – indeed, she marvelled at the ease with which obscenities tripped off her tongue and the speed with which a person could acquire rough edges.

Maria organized things so that she could prepare Carl's midday meal. Sharing out working hours presented no problem once she had come to an arrangement with the whores. At home she muzzled herself. No lewd remark – nothing of which she would have felt ashamed in Carl's presence – ever escaped her lips.

Her self-confidence returned. When Carl was kept down a class the second time, she felt strong enough to give his life a new direction: she took him out of school. This decision was, admittedly, preceded by consultations with Liesl and Lechner, but also with her fellow lavatory attendants. The whores knew that typesetting was a job with prospects.

That put paid to Carl's lessons with Samuel Gold. He still got an occasional opportunity to visit the bookshop at night, but time was far too short for an analysis, let alone an actual game. Carl had to limit himself to replacing a borrowed book on the shelf and pocketing another on Gold's recommendation.

His nights were spent with books on chess. As soon as he heard his mother's deep, regular breathing, he lit a candle in his bedroom and studied and analysed until he could not keep his eyes open any longer. He seldom slept more than four hours a night. Lechner, ever one to call a spade a spade, remarked on one of his visits that Carl looked as if he'd been "spewed up". Maria concurred. She suspected that the apprenticeship might be too much for him, and she was right. Carl was wholly unsuited to a skilled trade. It was not simply that he failed to distinguish between type sizes, estimate the distance between lines, and pick out the right characters, notably the different forms of "s" in Gothic script. Not a day went by without at least one completed stick of type slipping through his fingers and falling to the floor. This earned him some hearty slaps. The slaps became even heartier when he contrived to drop the composing stick into a drawerful of type. This not only ruined the work he had already completed but meant that the characters had to be sorted out and replaced in their correct compartments. The only thing that presented Carl with no problems was having to read type upside down and back to front. Sweeping the composing-room floor was a welcome chore. His overseer didn't bother to slap him for any shortcomings in that respect.

The overseer was a charitable type, fortunately for Carl, because another man might have done him an injury. It took only three months for the truth to sink in. The overseer informed Maria, quite bluntly, that he could not be bothered with Carl any longer: the boy would never make a compositor. Having towed the failed apprentice to Maria's door by his collar, he released him, turned on his heel without another word, and strode off.

Carl was delighted. He could now spend his mornings, too,

in Samuel Gold's back room. Gold informed his friends that there was a youngster in his shop who was well on the way to becoming a powerful player. They came, saw, and marvelled. The circumspect way in which this fourteen-year-old boy defended the trickiest positions was particularly exemplary.

Carl had no conception of his own ability. All he wanted, all that concerned and interested him, was to study the masters' games in Gold's bookshop. He was secretly infuriated when his mother once more wrested him away from this blissful existence. In conjunction with her fellow lavatory attendants, Maria had come to the conclusion that the best thing for Carl would be a course of commercial training.

The business school claimed his afternoons as well as his mornings. He read chess manuals under cover of his desk, but he managed to answer the teacher's questions. It did not worry him that most of what he said was sheer nonsense. His answers were designed to keep the teacher sweet, but that was the extent of his ambitions. He sat there leafing through his books and looking forward to next year's match between Gunsberg and Chigorin.

One morning, Carl skipped school. He sat down in the park with a book on endgames and waited for Gold to open his shop, then spent the whole day with him. He enjoyed himself so much, he reappeared outside the shop the very next day. It annoyed him that he hadn't hit on this idea earlier. Before a week was up, he had banished all thoughts of business school from his mind.

A letter from the governors informed Maria that they had been compelled to bar Carl Haffner from further attendance at the school because he had absented himself for several months without a valid excuse.

Maria marched off to see Gold. When Carl heard her voice he scuttled round the table in a panic, looking for somewhere to hide, and crept behind the armchair. Gold straightened his tie and went out into the shop. There Frau Haffner told him that he was blighting her son's career. It was despicable of him to have encouraged the boy to play truant. Did he not realize that Carl needed professional qualifications? How would he ever make his way in life? He could not shove pieces of wood around a board for the rest of his days. It was all Gold's fault. Gold was mentally deranged. "Have you no conscience? Don't you realize what you're doing?"

The bookseller tried to pacify her, but she would not listen. "But what if it's what he wants?" he cried in desperation.

Maria fell silent. Gold seized the opportunity to offer her a chair and retired to the back room to fetch two cups of coffee. Carl peeped out from behind the armchair. Gold signalled to him to stay under cover.

For the next half-hour, Gold explained to Maria how he envisaged Carl's future career. He began by stressing that he had never meant to dissuade Carl from attending school. The boy had always come of his own free will. He, Gold, had not asked any questions. That had been a mistake, admittedly, but he wasn't sure that it amounted to a serious misdemeanour. Why not? Gold lowered his voice. Because, he said, Maria's son was something quite exceptional.

He took a sip of coffee, trying to gauge what impression his words had made. Gold disliked talking. He found that one could get along quite well without words, both in life and at the chessboard. A year ago he would have spared himself this scene. He would have blushed, apologized to Maria, and sent Carl home. In the last few months, however, the boy's play had matured to an almost incredible extent. Gold felt it his duty to be the advocate of such talent.

"Frau Haffner, I mean you and Carl no harm, please believe that. I've been playing chess for thirty years. I have also, with the utmost interest, observed the development of the game for about as long. I've witnessed thirty years of its history, and I'm conversant with books on its history in previous centuries. There have been few talents to equal your son's. I myself have never seen its like in three decades."

Gold asked Maria if she minded the smoke from his cigar. He had the feeling that the worst of her anger had subsided. She blew on her coffee and eyed him with some impatience. Disconcerted once more by her gaze, the bookseller lost his thread. For a while he digressed into an aimless dissertation on the culture of the royal game that culminated in the assertion that chess was morally edifying. He pulled himself together with an effort.

"You don't play chess," he went on. "You find it incomprehensible that someone can sink all his energies in a chequered board. It depends on your point of view. Other people cannot fathom why a person paints pictures to no purpose, enjoys pulling teeth, or studies the Talmud. Don't misunderstand me: I appreciate your concern. Your son plays chess instead of troubling his head about school."

He clicked his tongue. "Your son plays chess instead of troubling his head about school," he repeated, stubbing out his cigar. "But have you ever watched him play? Have you seen the way his eyes caress the pieces? Are you aware of the enthusiasm, the gravity, the moral fervour he brings to the game? I'm half tempted to call him a priest of his fraternity. He's obsessed with chess – he loves it, and he's a strong player. I tell you, there isn't a chess player of his age in Vienna he could not beat."

The church bells seemed to underline Gold's words. A customer entered the shop. He rose to his feet.

"Your son, Frau Haffner, was born with an unrivalled talent. I don't know if either of us has the right to stand in the way of its development. Carl has a vocation – he possesses genius."

Maria could not summon up a reply. Her head was buzzing with all those big words. She mumbled her thanks, without really knowing why, and left. She was so bemused, she even forgot about Carl.

Having attended to his customer, Gold returned to the back room and summoned Carl from his hiding place.

"Don't let it go to your head," he growled. "I had to exaggerate like mad for your sake." He gently pinched the boy's ear. "And now, go home."

The next day's tap on the shutter came earlier than usual.

The old whores took Maria to task. They knew precisely what became of someone who hadn't had a decent education. Before she knew it, Carl would be running off to vaudeville theatres and "protecting" young actresses. Either that, or trying his luck at cards. Anyone like that was bound to come to a bad end. Carl was already halfway to prison. Maria ought to reflect on what she was doing.

Maria shrugged her shoulders and shook her head. Although the bookseller had not convinced her that Carl was putting his time to good use, he had blunted her determination to change anything. She wasn't blind, either. Only a monster could have failed to be moved by Carl's blissful expression as he set off for his chess tuition in the mornings. Maria preserved the hope that his craze for chess would one day subside of its own accord, and that he would become bored with the game – preferably before it was too late.

Months went by. One afternoon, Gold broke off early and sent Carl to ask his mother for permission to come home a little later than usual. He was just lowering the shutters when the boy returned. "We're going to a café," he announced.

Carl was very surprised to find that the café, too, had a back room. Arrayed in it were at least twenty tables, each of them adorned with a chessboard. Every board was occupied and every table thronged with spectators. Carl's heart beat faster. His eyes widened as he stared avidly at the boards.

Gold introduced him to one or two people. He shyly returned their salutations. Although everyone welcomed him in a friendly fashion, he was glad when a gentleman promptly challenged him to a game. Gold fetched a board. Carl's diffidence evaporated after a few moves. Here in this room, with its massive chandeliers, velvet-swathed tables and crowd of chess players, he felt no less at home than in Gold's bookshop.

He walked home in a kind of dream. The night sky winked and glittered overhead. For the first time ever, he had the feeling that the street lamps had been lit for him as well as everyone else. He felt an affinity with the promenaders and cabbies. Not only had he acquired a new status vis-à-vis the people in the street; there was something within him that could not have failed to arouse their envy. He was closer to them and further from them than ever before.

Gold accompanied him to the café for several months. One afternoon, when the boy suggested another visit, Gold said he didn't have the time – he had a business to run as well, after all – and told him to go on his own. Carl jibbed at this. He was afraid he wouldn't be welcome without Gold. The bookseller pooh-poohed his fears. Carl was talking nonsense, he said. He could go with an easy mind.

Carl prowled round the café for some time. Twice he went up to the door, and twice he beat a retreat. At last he plucked up courage and went in. He was warmly welcomed and challenged to a game at once. That evening spelt the end of his reluctance to pit himself against the café's leading players without the bookseller's moral support.

Carl's evenings at the café made him aware of the problem of earning a living. His pockets were empty, and it embarrassed him not to be able to afford a coffee. He was at the mercy of the head waiter, who could have had him thrown him out at any moment, and he could not bring himself to ask his mother for money.

So he looked for work and found employment with a large firm. During the day he delivered parcels, at night he warmed his bones in the café. The work was hard. In order to be able to sit in the café in peace, however, he dispensed with all creature comforts and even with his visits to the bookshop. Although it gave Maria no pleasure that her son spent half the night in coffee houses, her worries were substantially diminished by the fact that he was working for a firm.

It was at this time that the café received a visit from Englisch, a celebrated Viennese chess master. His attention was drawn to the youth whom no one could defeat. Englisch played several games with Carl and won none of them. He was flabbergasted to learn that Carl was only eighteen but had been patronizing the establishment for two years or so. "Why wasn't I told before?" he thundered. "Are you mad, gentlemen?" He turned to Carl. "Tomorrow evening, my young friend, you're coming to the Vienna Chess Club. You don't know the address? Someone will take you there."

Englisch managed to assemble the city's leading players at the chess club the following night. His sternly expressed opinions carried a great deal of weight, so all were eager to see the prodigy discovered by the Nestor of the Vienna Chess Club. Carl lived up to their expectations. Although he lost a few games, he played extremely well and defeated two of the strongest masters.

Carl was enrolled in the club the same night, his membership fee being waived in deference to his financial position. Englisch went around for days, beaming triumphantly and accepting congratulations on his keen eye for burgeoning talent. In Vienna's chess cafés, the name Haffner was uttered like a message of hope.

The following month, Samuel Gold emigrated to America. He explained to Carl that he had no wish to wait until pogroms like those in the east became a popular proceeding in Vienna as well. Carl, who had never heard the word pogrom before, found Gold's departure monstrous and incomprehensible. He accompanied his friend to the train that was to take him to Hamburg, whence he intended to sail to America.

Returning home, Carl closeted himself in his room and wept. He didn't go to work the next day. For a week he sobbed the nights away like a child. America . . . It might have been on another planet.

Gold had bequeathed him several crates of books and responsibility for the chess page in the *Allgemeine Sportzeitung*.

*

The members of the Vienna chess school took Carl under their wing. Though very strong players, the city's five or ten masters were not absolutely world-class. Their most fervent desire was that Vienna be recognized as the world's leading school, and in their view it was already verging on that status. No other country numbered as many strong players among its citizens. All the Vienna chess school needed was a truly great player – one who could hold his own against the four or five best in the world. And now, along had come this fellow Haffner. They resolved to build him up and teach him all they knew. In a year or two, when he equalled them in strength, he would be able to develop on his own and rise to the very top. Vienna would then, at long last, become the world's chess metropolis.

Carl was prevailed upon to give up his job. To provide him with a livelihood and enable him to devote himself entirely to chess, several masters relinquished their columns in various newspapers. They hardly troubled to consult him, but he would not have objected in any case.

Carl devoted himself to chess for as many as ten hours a day. He edited chess pages, wrote articles – he was a far from brilliant stylist, but nobody cared – and analysed and played with the masters of the Vienna Chess Club. Within three months of joining the club he was trouncing nearly all comers. He seemed to be growing stronger from day to day. So brilliant was his play that a match was arranged between Carl and Vienna's leading master, Georg Hummel – an unofficial event for which local patrons of the game put up a sizeable purse.

The first game ended in a draw. So did the second. Likewise the third. The fourth, fifth, sixth, seventh, eighth, ninth and ten games were also drawn. The Viennese masters took a photograph of Carl, signed the back, and mailed it without a word of explanation to a chess club in Prague, native city of the then world champion, Wilhelm Steinitz.

| 7 |

Accompanying Carl on the journey to Berlin were three of the Vienna Chess Club's masters – Fähndrich, Horak, and Wolf – and two assistant secretaries. Carl's companions, who were in high spirits, celebrated his victory in the fifth game for the umpteenth time. Horak, a hefty man with a pockmarked face, sprayed the compartment with champagne. If Fähndrich were to be believed, Carl was world champion already. In the excitement of the contest, Fähndrich had taken to calling Carl by his first name. "You've got him, Carl," he said, gripping the challenger's hand. "He'll break his teeth on you."

With an abstracted smile, Carl thanked Horak and Wolf for the toasts they lavished on him. He wasn't in the mood to celebrate. His euphoria of the last few days had subsided. Having spent a long time analysing the last game against Lasker, he knew that he had won only because of an inexplicably stupid blunder on the world champion's part. Lasker had more or less made him a gift of the point. It was a Pyrrhic victory, not that anyone but himself seemed to have noticed.

After travelling for three hours and sinking some twice that number of bottles, the assistant secretaries were feeling under the weather. Horak and Wolf were playing a blind game. They mumbled the moves at each other in a stupor and squabbled over an allegedly impossible manœuvre every few minutes. Fähndrich had fallen asleep. Carl longed for some fresh air. He stepped over one of the assistant secretaries, who had slumped to the floor, and left the compartment. In the corridor he opened a window and stuck his head out into the blast of air.

His nervousness suddenly returned. He had not felt scared during the contest so far. Having been immersed in analyses in the intervals between the almost daily games, he had had no time to brood. Now he had time and to spare.

His success in the first five games seemed quite unaccountable. He dreaded losing all five of the games that remained, cursed the whistling of the locomotive, the monotonous clickety-clack of the wheels underfoot, which were bringing him ever closer to the threat of defeat. He itched to apply the emergency brake.

Carl gave a start: someone had nudged his elbow. It was Anna, smiling warmly. "I overslept," she said. "I only caught the train by a whisker. How are you feeling?"

"Quite well, thanks."

"Yes, you look it. You're nice and pale in the face. Any room in your compartment? There's a lieutenant in mine – he's hell-bent on seducing me. I warned him he'd catch something, but he refuses to be deterred."

Carl turned pink with embarrassment. He indicated his compartment without looking at her. "All the seats are taken, I'm afraid. That's to say, perhaps . . ."

Anna put her head round the door, to be greeted by loud and enthusiastic applause. She shut the door again. "I see," she said. "So that's why you're looking out of sorts."

Horak and Wolf welcomed their female visitor in high

delight. They swiftly bore the assistant secretaries off to their sleepers with the conductor's help and offered Anna a window seat. She drank only two glasses of champagne, though Horak swore that a third would do her no harm, and fiercely defended her glass against the lurching onslaughts of his arm. Wolf and he did all they could to render her journey enjoyable, telling anecdotes and falling over themselves to be polite. Anna, who was very tickled, produced a pencil and paper. The result was her first atmospheric piece for Hummel.

Carl had ever-recurring visions of Lasker's hawklike countenance. He took off his shoes, but noticed the holes in his socks in the nick of time. Huddling up in his seat, he went to sleep.

At the station he was welcomed by an official from the Berlin Chess Club, who conveyed him and Fähndrich to the Hotel Kaiser by car. Rooms had been reserved for them there, whereas the other guests from Vienna had to find their own accommodation. The living expenses of the principals and their seconds were being met by the Berlin Chess Club. Baron von Rothschild was paying for Horak, Wolf, and the secretaries. As for Anna, her outgoings were covered by the *Neue Freie Presse*.

Carl had paid one previous visit to Berlin for the international tournament of 1897. He didn't think much of the place. Not knowing his way around in foreign parts, he had no time for any city but Vienna. That was why he declined Fähndrich's exuberant invitation to come for a stroll and closeted himself in his hotel room. Light and spacious, this contained a double bed and a fine, sturdy oak table on which to set out his chessboard and analysis manuscripts. The floor was carpeted, and there was even an adjoining WC. Carl had seldom been allotted such elegant quarters during a chess tournament.

He reviewed Lasker's openings in the second and fourth

games until a representative of the Berlin Chess Club came to collect him. They drove to the venue, the Hôtel de Rome, where Dr Lewitt, president of the Berlin Chess Club, welcomed Carl and Fähndrich and showed them the room in which the contest would take place. A platform had been erected in the centre. Spectators could come and go as they pleased but were forbidden to set foot on the platform itself.

Feeling sick with excitement, Carl stared at the platform as if it were a scaffold. Once Dr Lewitt had informed him of the time appointed for the next day's opening ceremony, he clumsily excused himself, pleading that he was tired from the journey and needed to rest. He had himself driven straight back to the Hotel Kaiser, where he hurried up to his room and locked the door as though fleeing from a fusillade on the stairs.

Late that night, Fähndrich knocked on the door. Carl opened it with his hair dishevelled and dark rings under his eyes.

"*Che cosa fai, maestro?* Come along, we must eat. Get a move on, or we'll be too late. What do you mean, you aren't hungry? Ridiculous! Well, are you coming? Really not? Very well, suit yourself. Take care you don't ruin your eyes."

Anna and the rest of the Viennese delegation were waiting in the lobby. Fähndrich told a hotel employee to ensure that Herr Haffner had a hot meal delivered to his room before the kitchen closed for the night. Until tomorrow, he said, that was as much as he could do for his pigheaded protégé.

Anna hurried upstairs. She scratched at the door and miaowed. Carl took his time. She went on miaowing. When there was still no sound of movement inside the room, the cat turned into a tiger and made as if to gobble up the doorhandle.

Carl opened the door. "What's the matter?" Anna demanded. "Do you intend to starve to death up here?"

"I'm not hungry."

"You haven't eaten all day – unless you've been nibbling on the sly, which I doubt. It's unhealthy and abnormal, going without food for so long. Come along now." She put out her hand.

"I'm fine. I still have things to do. Excuse me, I'm sorry."

Anna lowered her arm, never taking her eyes off his face. She had never seen such an expression before. Carl was looking at her, but whatever he was seeing at that moment had little to do with her. Anna was familiar with a painter's love of his art, a musician's ecstatic devotion to his instrument. She had witnessed the fervour with which wise men from the East put themselves into mysterious trances, and she was no stranger to the look of the drunk or demented. But Carl's expression differed entirely. It was a blend of obsession, fear, and melancholy: the obsession, not of an artist, but of a pathological invalid; the fear of a strictly disciplined dog, the melancholy of a blind man. With uncharacteristic diffidence, Anna bade him goodnight.

While Fähndrich and the others were patronizing establishments that were just suitable, in their opinion, for gentlemen accompanied by a lady, Carl was kneading his temples over the chessboard. In search of an improvement on the opening he had selected for the fourth game, he found it at half-past one in the morning. At half-past two he remembered the roast meat and vegetables that had been delivered to his door hours before. They were cold and congealed. He deposited the plate on the bed. Overcome once more by thoughts of Lasker's greatness, he almost vomited. The room was wreathed in smoke from innumerable cigarettes. He opened the window. Turning to the second game, he discovered an improvement on this variation at half-past four. After analysing Lasker's endgame a while longer, he realized that his teeth were chattering, and that he was shivering all over. He closed the window and fell asleep in his chair.

At breakfast in the well-lit, well-heated hotel dining-room, Fähndrich came out with one or two reminiscences of the previous night. Carl listened with only half an ear. Fähndrich had a thick head. He failed to notice that something was wrong with Carl until he had disposed of several rolls and cups of coffee. He saw the dark rings under his eyes, the twitching cheeks, the coffee spilt by an unsteady hand. "God Almighty!" he groaned. "You mean you came with us after all, and I don't remember?"

Fähndrich proceeded to castigate himself loudly. It was disgraceful, the way he'd neglected his duties as Carl's second. Instead of ensuring that his principal got a good night's rest, he had poured wine and liqueurs down his throat in sundry cabarets. The train journey must have scrambled his wits. He cursed the city's bad influence and his own irresponsibility. His remorse was such that Carl, whose stomach was churning with agitation, had to ply him with soothing words until it was time to go.

"But you haven't eaten anything again!" Fähndrich exclaimed. Carl raised both hands in a gesture of refusal and left the dining-room in double-quick time. Fähndrich wrapped some rolls in a napkin and hurried after him.

The Hôtel de Rome was crowded, but the crush was not as great as it had been in Vienna. Lasker was the local contender, after all, whereas few people in Berlin were familiar with Carl's face. He and Fähndrich had no difficulty in getting past the rope that cordoned off the speaker's lectern and the tables bearing the cold buffet. Dr Lewitt welcomed Carl and introduced his fellow organizers. Lasker, standing a little apart, was in conversation with Jacques Mieses. When Carl caught sight of his opponent's striking face, he felt his cheeks burn and his heart beat wildly. But Lasker, too, seemed unusually tense. He avoided Carl's eye when shaking hands. He didn't radiate the self-assurance that had characterized him in Vienna, thought Anna, who was fighting off her fatigue in the row of spectators immediately behind the rope. He looked somewhat sluggish and less confident than a week ago. Anna waved to Carl, but he didn't see her.

Dr Lewitt clapped his hands, and the murmur of voices died away. Having welcomed all present on behalf of the Berlin Chess Club and uttered some more civilities, he turned to Lasker. He was very proud of the speech he proceeded to deliver. He had written it himself, committed it to memory, and rehearsed it for days in front of a mirror.

"Esteemed Herr Dr Lasker, in Vienna, we saw you in an unwonted light. Please take it in good part, therefore, if I address you, a mathematician, in a language with which you are conversant, and if I juggle with one or two mathematical terms. You are here surrounded by chess enthusiasts eager to witness your achievements. We are dealing with two known quantities, and we propose to discover an unknown third, the future victor. Were we to seek him with the aid of the theory of probabilities, we might easily come to grief. I cannot refrain from thinking, in this regard, of the numerator into which your dangerous rival so skilfully coaxed you . . ."

Dr Lewitt went on to cite Feuerbach's theorem, spoke of parallels, and stressed that a straight line is the shortest route to success. Visibly flattered by his listeners' amusement, he gave a little bow and acknowledged the applause with a thin-lipped smile.

"Rather than stray from the strait and narrow, I shall now address myself to our second guest." Dr Lewitt commended Carl's modesty and his services as chess correspondent of the *Deutsche Schachzeitung*. He regretted the fact that Carl was not accompanied by Georg Hummel, that most genial of all the Viennese masters. Then he quoted from an article in which Carl had been summed up, years before, by the present world champion. "Haffner has sufficient ability for a world championship contest," Lasker had written, "but only the ability, nothing more. He is a man who likes a quiet life. He lacks the will to assert himself . . ."

That concluded Lewitt's introduction of the challenger.

Carl was not offended. He hadn't taken in a single word of the speeches. His shirt was clinging dankly to his back, and he could not feel his legs. All he wanted was to sit down at the board and get the game over. But then, at the mention of a gold watch, he pricked up his ears. Dr Lewitt announced that Mr Hugo Jackson, the proprietor of an arts and crafts shop in Berlin, had donated a gold watch for presentation to the winner of the match.

A shiver of emotion ran down Carl's spine as he pictured himself making a gift of the watch to Lina. The next moment, however, it occurred to him that he had no prospect of winning the watch. He started to sweat again. His ears burned, his stomach heaved.

The rope was removed for the duration of the buffet. Several Berlin dignitaries paid their respects to Carl. Anna and Horak joined them. Although Carl shook hands with everyone, he was glassy-eyed and wholly unresponsive. Anna doubted if he could tell one face from another. A roll pressed on him by Fähndrich was going stale in his hand. Suddenly his expression changed. Dashing over to the buffet, he drank three or four glasses of fruit juice in as many minutes. Anna exchanged a puzzled glance with Fähndrich, who shrugged his shoulders. Carl fled to the lavatory, whence Fähndrich managed to extricate him just in time for the game.

The crisis was surmounted. As in Vienna, Carl's nerves were soothed by the routine alternation of game and almost unremitting analysis. He had no time to dwell on the possibility of defeat, and his abidingly strong play made its own contribution: he drew the sixth and seventh games. People found this almost more surprising than his victory in Vienna. The general assumption had been that the Austrian challenger would go to pieces in Berlin, but the contrary happened. One press commentator jocularly asserted that Haffner seemed to have grown two inches since the start of the championship.

Every train brought more chess masters, official correspondents, or curious spectators to Berlin. The match turned into a festival as the international chess fraternity foregathered in the German capital. Suddenly, everyone wanted to witness this sensational contest. Bets of increasing size were laid. Although there was some reluctance to forecast the exact score, Haffner was considered unlikely to win. Most people predicted that Lasker would shake off his peculiar lethargy and win at least two of the three remaining games, but there were a few who at least toyed with the thought of a new world champion. Carl Haffner, world chess champion . . . The idea was as incongruous as a labour leader on the Austro-Hungarian throne.

The wording of the telegrams Anna received from Georg Hummel was so muddled that she wondered, half seriously, if the contest was unhinging her employer's mind. Some of these missives were addressed to Carl, but she refrained from passing them on. Not exhortations in the strict sense, they contained fanciful absurdities that would, at most, have distracted Carl or made him nervous. Hummel not only referred to Julius Caesar and Alexander the Great, but was presumptuous and extravagant enough to cable a bombastic essay on the Viennese chess tradition. As for the telegram in which he married Caissa, the goddess of chess, to the anarchist Michael Bakunin, neither Anna nor Horak nor Wolf could understand how it had slipped past the censor.

A few hours after Carl had drawn the eighth game, too, a messenger boy – sneeringly, so she thought – handed Anna yet another telegram. It read: "Dear Telegraphist, please draw a fat, tipsy, grinning man smoking a cigar and brandishing his fist – stop – Make the fist really huge – stop – Hurrah!"

| 8 |

The day of the ninth game, the edition of the *Neue Freie Presse* containing Anna's account of the train journey reached Berlin. Hummel had not altered a comma of it.

The assistant secretaries put the newspaper down and slunk off. Horak brandished it in Anna's face. "What's the meaning of this?" he hissed, puce in the face. "*At a late hour, one of the masters in the party invited the author of this article to visit the sleeping car . . .* What are you insinuating? I wanted to see how our secretaries were faring, you know that perfectly well!"

"I know nothing of the kind," Anna replied amiably. "But there's nothing in the article to suggest otherwise."

"Nor is there any reference to the secretaries! Everyone will think . . ."

"You didn't mention the secretaries. You made eyes at me and tried to talk me into an excursion to the sleeping car. I wrote no more than that. Less, in fact."

Horak swore like a trooper. Without looking at Anna, he stuffed the newspaper into a wastepaper basket and turned on his heel. Highly amused, she watched him march briskly out of the lobby of the Hôtel de Rome, where they waited each morning for their mail and newspapers. She wondered how he would react to her piece on their nocturnal tour of the cabarets, which had yet to appear.

She certainly did not mean her reports to harm him and the others. Hummel had asked for her personal impressions of the trip, and she was supplying them. He had even wired his congratulations on each article. She wrote what she saw, making discreet allusions that gave a glimpse of what was going on behind the scenes. Horak had evidently expected her to preserve a kind of comradely silence. It never occurred to him that she might also feel some sympathy for a fourteen-year-old Polish belly dancer. That became clear to him when he read her piece on their night out together.

Anna had spent only the first two days in the company of the Viennese delegation. Thereafter she explored the city unescorted by chess masters. She visited exhibitions and attended concerts, went to the theatre and watched a football match. She wrote about everything, and not just for Hummel's benefit. A friend had given her the address of a socialist debating club, where she made the acquaintance of a printer who acted as her guide on ensuing nights.

Anna did not neglect her work for Hummel in spite of all her other interests. She spoke with Dr Lewitt and other members of the Berlin chess fraternity, with Lasker himself and most of the masters who ringed the platform in the Hôtel de Rome. In so doing she tried to steer them away from the subject of chess and on to more general topics. She wanted to discover if such men had anything in common apart from the game.

The majority were reserved by nature. Where responsiveness to the world outside the sixty-four squares was concerned, individuals like the shallow, pleasure-loving Horak and Wolf were exceptions. The masters Anna interviewed, who hailed from all parts of the world, had little to contribute to any conversation dealing with matters other than openings, middle games, and endgames. While play was in progress they gazed at the board or the man-sized demonstration boards, puffed at their cigars, conveyed the fruits of their deliberations to their neighbours in a whisper, and made only disjointed allusions to their personal welfare and private circumstances. That was understandable, given the prevailing excitement. Even when Lasker and Carl had completed a game, however, it remained impossible to extract a sensible remark from the spectators. They veiled themselves in tobacco smoke and argued over this or that manœuvre. The situation was no better when Anna encountered one of them hours later. She decided to take the bull by the horns.

"Tell me, Master Lipke," she asked, all innocent, "how much does a litre of milk cost?"

Master Lipke apologized with artless courtesy and advised her to consult one of the organizers. She put the same question to another master. He stared at her as if she had asked him why hydrochloric acid wasn't flowing from the frozen fountain outside the hotel. The third shrugged his shoulders, the fourth offered to stand her a glass of milk, the fifth named an astronomical sum.

Anna marvelled anew every day at the ability of these men to regard a chessboard as the sole reality. They were as single-minded as children. Their emotions were dominated by chess, and chess alone. Many of the masters were married, but Anna went so far as to doubt the validity of their marital state. These men had dedicated themselves, heart and soul, to a game. Their devotion was blind and unconditional, exclusive and fanatical. They served their art more zealously than any sportsman, physician or academic Anna had ever met. There was nothing wrong with that, in itself, but Anna could not help feeling that they had devoted themselves to the game with such passion because they were deficient in something else.

Lasker she excepted. The world champion made a sound and stable impression. He was cultured, sophisticated, witty. His verdicts on European politics were quite as perceptive as those of any expert commentator. He knew as much about physical phenomena as he did about herbal remedies. He had travelled widely, and Anna sensed from all he said that he had kept his eyes open in the process. At the same time, he was never anything but affable and refrained from lecturing his listeners like a headmaster. Conversing with him was a pleasure. Where most of the other masters were concerned, Anna felt as if she were trying to wring secrets from mentally disturbed children.

She found it just as arduous to talk with Carl. On their first encounter she had succeeded in discovering something of the chess player's human side. In Berlin he behaved as if he were under the influence of inhibitory drugs. He was monosyllabic and never went out at nights; instead he stewed in his room and spent hours moving pieces around the board until it was time for the next game.

Anna wondered if there was a woman in Carl's life. She doubted it – indeed, she suspected that women held no attraction for him. There was something about his manner, his way of addressing and looking at her, that seemed to betray this. She could not be sure, of course, nor did it matter to her much, except as part of a mosaic and as one particular aspect of his character. Anna's principal motive for undertaking an excursion into the world of chess had always been, and still was, to fathom this peculiar individual – this person who disliked being a nuisance and was contesting a world championship against his will.

Shortly before the ninth game, Carl sent Lina a postcard – his invariable custom when playing away from home: "Dear Lina, I'm well. I should be back in Vienna by the beginning of March. Love, Carl."

He never wrote more than that. Not a word about the current state of the match or tournament. That wouldn't have interested her, he felt. The postcard's sole function was to show that he was thinking of her. He longed to hint at his intention of giving her a present, but he refrained, afraid that he would fail to keep his promise and disappoint her. Many were the times he revelled in the mental picture of himself knocking at Lina's door with the gold watch in his hand. Then it occurred to him that Lasker might well give him a terrible drubbing in the last two games, and that his sister, who was doubtless daydreaming over the keyboard in Vienna at that moment, would never set eyes on the watch at all. That thought cut him to the quick.

He entrusted the postcard to the porter at the Hotel Kaiser. Rather than put the organizers to any trouble, he dispensed with the car that was waiting for him and set off for the Hôtel de Rome on foot. He wasn't feeling too bad, and his fear of defeat had largely subsided. Even if he lost the last two games, he would have given a good account of himself. Besides, he was no longer so certain that he *would* lose both games. One, beyond a doubt, but he might contrive to draw the other. In that event, Lasker would still be world champion, but without having won the match.

The Berlin Chess Club's car puttered past. The chauffeur tooted and Fähndrich, who was ensconced in the back, waved.

Carl was shivering with cold in his thin frock coat. He warmed himself by swinging his arms as he walked. The sun was shining, the snow on the road melting. The clatter of horses' hoofs sounded far less muffled than it had a few days ago. Carl was beginning to understand the Berlin dialect he could hear on all sides. He checked the time by a church clock. A snowball slammed into the back of his neck. Children's laughter rang out behind him. He didn't turn round, merely walked on faster.

When he turned into the street in which the Hôtel de Rome was situated and saw the crowd outside, he suddenly became aware of an incredible fact: today might see him gain the world championship. Before the day was out, he might have succeeded Steinitz and Lasker to become the third world chess champion in history. If he won the ninth game, Lasker would be unable to overhaul him in the tenth. A victory today, and there would be no one above him in the chess hierarchy.

Positively dazed by this realization, he elbowed his way through the throng like a man in a dream. The exhortations of his Viennese friends impinged on his consciousness as little as the spectators' applause and the arbiter's ritual words of introduction. He shook a ghostly hand and settled himself at the board. The clock whose ticking he could hear was made of gold.

For the Viennese delegates, the hours that followed were nerve-racking in the extreme. Carl did not play with his usual caution. After the opening he made a blunder that cost him a pawn. Not once did he get up to stretch his legs, and the intensity of the opponents' combined gaze was such that Anna would not have been surprised to see the table break in half beneath it. In excited whispers, the masters ringing the platform debated whether the lost pawn had already clinched the game in Lasker's favour.

After a few hours the game was discontinued and adjourned. Lasker, with his tie loosened, jumped up and hurried out of the hotel. Carl, too, exchanged only a few words with the arbiter for courtesy's sake before leaving by a rear entrance. The masters unanimously agreed that Haffner had his back to the wall. The game was as good as lost.

Carl insisted on being left alone until the resumption. Undeterred, Fähndrich appeared outside his room with a plateful of chicken casserole and a bottle of burgundy and hammered on the door. Two hotel guests complained of the noise. One of them, mistaking Fähndrich for a member of the staff, asked to be brought a glass of water and a sleeping pill. Fähndrich replied in such an atrocious Austrian dialect that the man lapsed into startled silence. Finally, he rattled the doorhandle. The door was unlocked, the room empty, the chessboard nowhere to be seen.

Carl tiptoed into his room late that night, shoes in hand. For peace and privacy's sake, he had taken refuge in a coffee house.

He slept for three hours until awakened by his second. From then on, Fähndrich never let him out of his sight. After supervising Carl's morning ablutions with a wary eye, he took the budding world champion's hand and led him into the dining room, where he compelled him to eat a substantial breakfast. When Carl proposed to walk to the Hôtel de Rome, he was seized and hustled into the car without a word. Having delivered Carl to the platform and gone to join Horak and Wolf, Fähndrich cast his eyes up to heaven and crossed himself with an exaggerated flourish. The Viennese masters eyed each other in silence. They all knew what was at stake.

The game took so exciting a turn that some spectators could not bear to watch. They hurried out of the hall and into the street, where they paced to and fro and followed developments at second hand. Sensational reports came to their ears. Haffner was once more doing justice to his reputation as the best defensive player in the world. Lasker charged his opponent's position and essayed some tactical pinpricks, but in vain: Haffner was impregnable. The ninth game, too, ended in a draw. Fähndrich whooped with delight when peace was concluded. Only one more draw was required – only one more undecided game.

9

After his match against Hummel, Carl was invited to a tournament in Leipzig the following year, 1894. He came eleventh out of eighteen – not an outstanding result, but he had at least confirmed his talent.

He gained a more important success before the tournament took place. His mother refused to let him go. "To Leipzig by yourself?" she exclaimed in horror. "On the map, with your finger, maybe, but that's all!"

So inflexible was her opposition that, a few days later, Carl called on Englisch, who had extracted the invitation from Leipzig, to say that he would not be taking part.

"What? Stay at home because your mother objects? Are you a regular churchgoer, or something?"

Englisch talked to Carl as he might have addressed a mentally retarded child. When he saw that he was in earnest, he patted him on the shoulder. "Never fear, you'll be allowed to go."

That evening, a smart carriage driven by a liveried coachman pulled up outside Carl's home. It was Englisch, come to call on his mother accompanied by two distinguished chess enthusiasts, the industrialist Anton Trebitsch and Prince Hohenstein. They led off with a gift hamper and two armfuls of flowers.

"We thought you might like to know the kind of company your son keeps."

Having introduced himself and his companions, Englisch came straight to the point. In soothing tones, he informed Maria that Carl would not be travelling to Leipzig on his own. Chess Masters Hummel and Zinkl, respectable gentlemen both, would ensure that Carl lacked for nothing on the trip. Supervising a well-brought-up young man of twenty was not, after all, an impossible task. In any case, he himself, together with Messrs Trebitsch and Hohenstein would guarantee her son's welfare.

Englisch expatiated on Carl's talent and spoke of him as the future world champion. When he went on to rhapsodize about young people and their cherished dreams, Maria put her hands over her ears.

"Thank you," she said. "Thanks very much, that'll do. He can go, but please don't imagine it's your fine words that have changed my mind. In my line of work, one learns to treat flowery phrases like smells: they're just hot air. As long as someone looks after the boy, I've no objection to him playing that pointless game in Leipzig for once."

In the carriage, Englisch debated what Frau Haffner's line of work could possibly be. He resolved to ask Carl, but he'd forgotten by the time he got back to the Vienna Chess Club.

After his eleventh place at Leipzig, Carl was invited to the grand tournament at Hastings in 1895, the strongest in chess history. Those present included the dethroned world champion Wilhelm Steinitz, his successor Emanuel Lasker, the world championship aspirants Siegbert Tarrasch and Mikhail Chigorin, the English élite trio of Bird, Burn, and "Black Death" Blackburne, and many other eminent players. Carl managed to draw against

Tarrasch and Steinitz and actually defeated Harry N. Pillsbury, who won first prize. His ninth place out of twenty-two participants, half of them positive giants of the chessboard, was a sensation second only in magnitude to Pillsbury's success.

At the ensuing tournament in Nuremberg, Carl's equal seventh place earned him his very first prize money, two hundred Reichsmarks. Carl had never seen, far less possessed, so much money in his life. He gave all but twenty marks of it to his mother. Maria, who was genuinely delighted on his behalf, raised no objection when he set off for another tournament immediately afterwards. At Budapest he shared fourth place with Janowski. Back in Vienna once more, he played a six-master tournament in which he came second to Janowski, a psychopathic gambler. He retired to bed for three whole weeks after that. Though not ill in the clinical sense, he had shed eighteen pounds of his already meagre body weight in the course of the tournament. Sheer exhaustion had driven him to bed.

The Viennese masters were alarmed by this. A robust constitution was essential to any chess master desirous of getting to the very top. Many games required one to tussle for up to eight hours, and there were tournaments in which thirty games had to be played, one a day. No one who physically flagged had any prospect of attaining pre-eminence. Malicious tongues in the Viennese masters' second division were already wagging. "He'll never make world champion," it was said. "There's not enough meat on him."

Carl realized that he would have to husband his strength, so he changed his style. More safety-conscious than ever, he drew a large number of games in short order. The trouble was, this wholly logical strategy made it difficult for him to win a first-class tournament. It was a long time before he did win one, too, even though no international player of repute cast doubt on the young man's exceptional talent.

In the spring of 1898 a memorable tournament was held in Vienna to mark the fiftieth anniversary of Emperor Franz Joseph's accession to the throne. Thirty-six games had to be played, and Carl came fifth, thereby consolidating his reputation as Austria's strongest player. It was at this very juncture that Georg Hummel and his circle thought they detected a lack of definite improvement in their youthful prospect's play. Unable to discern any progress in his understanding of the game, they debated its cause. They forbore to question Carl himself, nor could he have given them an answer. In fact, the Viennese masters were partly to blame for his stagnation.

Until a certain night in the winter of 1897, Carl remained a kind of chess automaton. It was not that events remote from the chequered board left him cold; it was simply that he managed to shut his eyes to them. His world was the pyramid of chess players. He had no desire to stand at its apex; he wanted to carve himself a comfortable niche at his existing level and do nothing but play chess for the rest of his days. He could have been asked about the intricacies of chess in his own or any other language, and the purpose of such questions would have eluded him – until that December night, when he happened to be in Vienna and, by an even greater coincidence, not at the chess club but at home with his mother.

They were at supper when they heard a knock. Carl, who opened the door, found himself confronted by a woman holding a little girl by the hand. Possibly somewhat younger than his mother and afflicted with a tic in her left eye, she stared at him in a strangely disconcerted way and timidly asked to see Frau Haffner.

Carl invited the pair to come in. The woman's tic became even more pronounced as she shook hands with Maria. She introduced herself as the sister of Leopoldine Bauer, who had died twelve years earlier, and the little girl as her daughter. Carl, staring at his mother, wondered if the tic was infectious. The next moment, Maria seized his arm and thrust him towards the door. He lingered outside, straining his ears in bewilderment, but Maria came out and shooed him away. Her eyes were flashing with a kind of blind rage that was new in his experience.

He waited outside the house. Fifteen minutes later the woman emerged with the child. Her rouge was smudged. "Please come to see us," she begged. She told Carl her address and squeezed his hand. He walked once round the block. Then, feeling wrung out, he returned to the apartment.

"Who was that?"

Maria refused to answer. He persisted, but her response was a furious outburst of frightening intensity, followed by a paroxysm of weeping. Carl put his arms around her. "Has something bad happened?"

She shook her head and wept until skeins of saliva oozed from her lips. It was a long time before she calmed down, and even then she refused to talk about the woman and the child.

The next day, Carl hurried to the address he'd been given in Zimmermanngasse. There he learned that the little girl's name was Lina, and that she was his half-sister. Her aunt, who had brought her up, told him the story of Adalbert and Leopoldine.

Carl spent several hours with his new-found relations. Lina's aunt had fallen on such hard times that she didn't know where to turn. In desperation, she had risked calling on Adalbert's widow, only to be turned away.

Carl brought the Bauers all the money he could spare – which was more than he could spare. He bought them food and sweets, clothes and cooking utensils, and prefaced every visit to the Bauers by touring the shops in search of a doll for Lina. His mother remained ignorant of the whole business.

Years later, Lina wrote him a letter. Maria put the envelope, which bore Lina's name on the back, in his room, but she never mentioned the subject.

Carl could not have explained the intricacies of chess even then, after making his sister's acquaintance, but he had at least grasped its practical purpose.

He was somewhat distracted from his fanatical study of chess theory by something else, namely, the Viennese masters' social conventions and the erudition that underlay them. Carl had been struck, when he first joined the Vienna Chess Club, by the singular remarks with which the masters embellished their moves in countless informal games. He assumed it to be an esoteric jargon of some kind. In fact, the members of the Vienna Chess Club seasoned every conversation, whether at the chessboard or away from it, with witty comments in various languages ranging from French to Latin, Greek, and Hebrew. They quoted the literary classics, imitated characters from stage plays, sang arias, and employed technical terms from the fields of medicine, chemistry, or sport. It was taken for granted at the chess club that a member could grasp the others' allusions and reply in the same vein.

Carl was uncomprehending. Although no one tried to rub his nose in his ignorance, he developed an inferiority complex. That was why, for the first time since his school days, he picked up a book that had nothing to do with chess. He read ten selected works within the space of a year. "In essence," Hummel had confided to him, unasked, "world literature consists of no more than ten books. The rest are redundant – no one would miss them."

After reading the said ten books and – albeit less zealously and only on occasion – several others, Carl joined in the chess club's conversations for initiates. If his opponent made an ambiguous remark, he would respond with a quotation that seemed to him to fill the bill.

Chess was not the only game played in the elegant rooms of the Vienna Chess Club. Tarot was a universal craze. Carl, who learnt the game simply by watching, developed such a liking for it that he used to play tarot with the problemists Soyka and Steiner at a coffee house every Wednesday evening. Sometimes they were late. That was when he found it could be very pleasant to sit in a café and do nothing or read a newspaper – not play chess, at all events. He was discovering how to relax.

As a result of this digression into a life outside the world of strategy and variations, Carl's chess made little progress. Many people wrote him off as a candidate for the world championship. An unofficial list of world rankings compiled by some English chess theorists placed him fifteenth at the end of 1897, fifteenth again the following year, and fourteenth the year after that. Carl was more than content with this. He failed to understand his Viennese confrères' gentle admonitions and dismissed their half-hearted allusions to Lasker's title. He had no need to become world champion, he was satisfied with his present status. He not only wrote for over a dozen chess periodicals but, in 1899, was appointed co-editor of the *Deutsche Schachzeitung*. This work fulfilled him. He kept up his tarot sessions, went for walks with his mother, took his leisure in coffee houses, played tournaments. Every visit he paid to Zimmermanngasse filled him with anticipation. He was especially delighted when Lina asked him questions – when she came to him with her little problems and, without prompting, recounted the events of the foregoing days. He was touched by her faith in him. Had she requested it, he would have done his best to build her a palace.

Carl could not, of course, have contemplated such a costly undertaking. His expenditure on Lina was a heavy drain on his purse. He had to think very carefully before travelling to a tournament, because failure could have spelt ruin. Carl's eyes were opened to the precarious financial circumstances even of successful tournament players by an incident that occurred during the London tournament of 1899.

Pillsbury, the American chess master, gave a display in front of fifty spectators. He sat at a card table and played whist with three other people. Simultaneously, he played ten games of chess against persons who had paid for the privilege of pitting themselves against the great Harry Nelson Pillsbury. He did not play those games by getting up from the whist table and scanning his opponents' row of boards in turn; he played them blind.

At the same time, Pillsbury got the spectators to hand him fifty numbered slips of paper, each bearing a five-word sentence. He read each sentence once and laid the slip aside. When a number was called, he recited the relevant sentence. After that he repeated all fifty sentences backwards. He did not make a single mistake. He not only won at the whist table; he won all the blind games, which he continued to play without interruption while performing his trick with the slips of paper.

Two English professors asked Pillsbury for an encore. They handed him a list of words designed to overtax his memory. Pillsbury looked at the sheet of paper and returned it. "Forwards or backwards?" he asked. Without waiting for an answer, he reeled off the list: "Antiphlogistic, periosteum, Taka-Diastase, plasmin, threlkeld, streptococcus, staphylococcus, micrococcus, plasmodium, Mississippi, Freiheit, Philadelphia, Cincinnati, athletics, no war, Etchenerg, American, Russian, philosophy, Piet Potgieter's Rost, salmagundi, Oomisillecootsi, Bangmamvate, Haffner's neck, Manzinyama, theosophy, catechism, Madjesoomalops."

Without faltering, he recited the words backwards as well as forwards. The next day he repeated them to prove that he genuinely knew them by heart.

Carl, who had attended the performance at Pillsbury's invitation, was as staggered by it as everyone else, but he felt concerned for Pillsbury's health. Such intense concentration could not be mentally beneficial. He asked the American why he took such risks. "I need the money," was Pillsbury's candid explanation. "If I didn't give at least one performance a week, I'd have to eat chess books."

In 1900, Carl shared first prize with Pillsbury at Munich. The Viennese masters breathed a sigh of relief. A tournament victory at last! Carl had just turned twenty-six. "It's his breakthrough," Hummel predicted. "This is just the start!"

But it wasn't his breakthrough. Despite the Viennese masters' exhortations, Carl did not play anywhere near as many tournaments as they would have liked, and there was another long interval before he won again. At Cambridge Springs in 1904, when he once more set tongues wagging, few still believed him to be a serious candidate for the supreme title. What drew attention to him at that Pennsylvania spa was less his strong play than a singular incident.

While playing the subsequent winner of the tournament,

the American master Frank J. Marshall, Carl got into difficulties. He and his opponent stood chatting when the game was adjourned. Marshall asked Carl what he thought of his position. "Not much," Carl replied. "I shall probably have to resign before long."

At the resumption, the arbiter opened the envelope containing Carl's sealed move, carried it out on the board, and started the clock. Marshall had yet to appear, but that didn't matter in view of all the time he had accumulated. Carl amused himself by watching the games in progress on other boards. He talked with Lasker and other masters, freshened up, and did some more kibitzing. The arbiter came over to him.

"Mr Marshall still isn't here. He'll be out of time in a quarter of an hour."

Carl was worried now. Had Marshall misunderstood him? They'd been speaking English, a language he did not know well. Perhaps Marshall had understood him to say that he had resigned the game and would not be returning at all. He would then be declared the winner, but how embarrassing to score a point in that way!

The arbiter came up to him again. Only another five minutes.

Carl hurried over to the table. The minute hand was already lifting the flag on Marshall's clock. If it fell, the hour would be up and Carl would have won. Three more minutes to go. Two more . . .

Carl stopped the clock in token of resignation and returned all the pieces to their starting positions with the exception of Marshall's king, which he placed in the middle of the board. This informed all who passed by that the American had won.

Marshall, who breezed into the hall half an hour later, looked at the board, saw his victorious king, and, unwitting, shook

Carl's hand. Then he studied the tournament table. Carl said not a word about the circumstances in which he had resigned. As far as he was concerned, that was that. He did not give the matter another thought until reminded of it at the closing ceremony.

Carl had come equal sixth out of sixteen competitors. When reading out his name, the tournament organizer described him as "the man who played the fairest move ever seen".

Carl's sportsmanlike conduct in the game against Marshall enhanced his popularity still further. He was, without doubt, the most respected master in the world. Friendly and courteous in his dealings, unfailingly modest in manner, and so obliging that he would even bring his opponents a cup of tea or coffee when they were pondering a move or running short of time, Carl was universally liked. No one ever had a bad word to say about him. Not even the most monomaniacal chess master could speak ill of a man who hardly dared reject the offer of a draw for fear of hurting his opponent's feelings.

In Vienna, Carl's fair play against Marshall was taken for granted. What excited the masters in Georg Hummel's circle was another incident at Cambridge Springs: Carl had defeated Lasker. The Viennese champion had proved superior to the world champion in a head-to-head – it was the talk of every chess café in the imperial capital.

Regardless of the fact that Carl had no impressive tournament victories to his credit, Hummel began to ponder aloud in his chess column on the prospect of a world championship contest between Haffner and Lasker. His proposal met with no great response. Few people thought the frail Viennese capable of defeating Lasker under match conditions, especially as Haffner himself disclaimed any ambition to engage in such a contest.

Hummel, who regarded himself as Carl's chess guardian, declared his pronouncements null and void. "If it comes to it," he wrote, "Haffner will play. He owes it to the chess fraternity."

Needless to say, the chess fraternity had no intention of calling in that debt. There were worthier aspirants, notably Tarrasch and Pillsbury, Marshall, Janowski, and Maroczy of Hungary. Maroczy forbore to challenge Lasker for a reason that made everyone sit up and take notice: his avowed belief that Lasker was unbeatable by himself or anyone else. As for Pillsbury, his play steadily declined in strength, no one knew why. He was thirty-four years old when he died in 1906. What occasioned his untimely death was not the intellectual haemorrhaging of his ideas, but the syphilis he had caught from a prostitute after playing a brilliant game at the St Petersburg tournament of 1896.

That left Marshall, Tarrasch, and Janowski. First, Lasker tackled Marshall and demolished him eight-nil. The following year brought a long-awaited duel between Lasker and his fellow countryman Tarrasch. Once again, Lasker scored a clearcut victory. After the world champion had gone on to wipe the floor with Janowski, voices other than Maroczy's were heard proclaiming the futility of any challenge to Lasker's supremacy. The world champion played like a being from another planet.

It was during these years that something unexpected happened – unexpected, that is to say, by any master who did not drink his coffee in Vienna: Carl Haffner's play became stronger. He triumphed at Ostende in 1906 and won the Vienna and Prague tournaments in 1908. Of the thirty-eight games he played in the latter year he lost only one. No master in the world had ever performed such a feat under comparable circumstances.

His successes furnished Hummel with additional arguments. This time, the only people who opposed him were those who thought Lasker invincible. The Vienna Chess Club sent Lasker an official challenge, and the world champion acknowledged the validity of the challenger's claims.

Carl learned from the press that his negotiations with Lasker were already far advanced. It seemed that the match was to consist of thirty games covering Vienna, Berlin, Stockholm, London, and New York. This plan fell through because it proved impossible to raise the money for an event of such magnitude. Carl was surprised to read in the *Neue Freie Presse* that Lasker and he had jointly signed a circular letter headed "To the Chess World", but that not even this had done the trick.

In the autumn of 1909, Hummel marched into the analysis room of the Vienna Chess Club, slapped Carl on the back, and boomed, "We've done it!" Ten games divided equally between Vienna and Berlin, Lasker to retain the world championship in the event of a tie.

Carl sighed. He nodded slowly and gravely. "I suppose I should thank you," he said in a hoarse voice. The prospect of this dreaded match burned his innards like fire.

Carl watched Lina grow up with warm-hearted affection. When he asked her what she wanted most of all, she confessed that she dreamed of playing the piano. Carl paid for her piano lessons. Meantime, he scrimped and saved until he had amassed enough money for a second-hand concert grand. He did not mind limiting himself to one meal a day and wearing a thin, threadbare jacket in winter. The day on which the piano was delivered meant more to him than any victory ceremony.

Lina's teacher, who was impressed by her talent, offered to

introduce her to important people and obtain her some professional engagements. Lina thanked her but declined. She had no wish to play in public, she did not consider herself good enough. If she played at all, it was only for Carl and her aunt, and she would sometimes make an exception for a girlfriend. Carl loved these recitals and deplored his sister's refusal to play in public. In his estimation, Lina should have performed in the presence of the emperor.

After her aunt died, Lina began to give piano lessons herself. She found it embarrassing to take so much money from Carl and wanted to earn her own living.

She developed into such an excellent teacher that she was soon having to turn pupils away. Her income was enough to live on. Though not by any means well-off, she earned more than her brother. Despite this, Carl continued to slip banknotes into her money box. He wanted Lina to be able to buy any clothes and jewellery she pleased, heedless of the fact that she seldom wore jewellery and never spent money on smart attire. Her only concern, apart from her passion for playing the piano, was the welfare of Carl and her women friends. She had no interest in anything else.

Money shuttled back and forth between Lina and Carl without their realizing it. Carl would surreptitiously slip a banknote into Lina's money box. Lina would open the box weeks later, rejoice to see how much she had saved, and stuff some notes into Carl's pocket. Carl would come across them weeks or months later, fail to remember how they got there, and insert them in Lina's money box. Quite appreciable sums passed between them over the years.

| 10 |

Lasker claimed a two-day break before the tenth and last game. While encouraging telegrams were arriving at the hotel reception desk from all over the world, Austria in particular, Carl spent the time dashing to and fro between the chess table in his room and the lavatory next door. Although he ate next to nothing, his digestion was out of kilter and his intestines were rumbling with unprecedented excitement. In the end he borrowed Fähndrich's pocket chess set so as to be able to analyse while seated on the pan. Fähndrich tried to wrest him away from the fug of the hotel room and begged him to come for a walk. He was so insistent that Carl finally consented. "This evening," he promised.

Carl never went for that walk because his second was in no condition to chivvy him out into the street. That afternoon, Fähndrich cracked under the strain of his responsibilities. Slouching into a tavern near the hotel, he drank a schnapps to relieve the tension. Although aware of warning signs after draining his third glass, he was past pulling himself together. By nightfall he was entertaining the landlord and his astonished customers to some sentimental Viennese ballads. Later still, he lamented his moral decline, burst into tears, and slid to the floor. As luck would have it, the landlord knew where the grief-stricken Austrian was staying, so he and the hotel porter carried him up to his room. Fähndrich was suddenly overcome with mirth during this operation. "A goo' thing the Feiertanz woman ishn't here," he burbled, and, "We're going to be world champions!" He laughed so uproariously that the porter wondered whether to summon a doctor. Only when he was fast asleep did the man return to his desk and confine himself to sending a bellhop to his room once an hour, armed with a pail.

Carl was unaware of these events. Although he stopped analysing, he hardly slept a wink all night. He was haunted by thoughts about the forthcoming duel – for instance, whether he would make a worthy world champion if he drew the last game, in which case the contest would have been decided by his chance victory in the fifth. Or, what the world championship signified: prestige, a place in the annals of chess, challenges by other masters, and – of this there was no doubt – a return match against Lasker.

Carl's restless night was an alternation of bed and lavatory accompanied by recurrent mental images of the gold watch.

The next morning, on the eve of the decider, he went out immediately after breakfast. After a while he found a café whose exterior appealed to him – a favourable impression that was confirmed once he had gone through the revolving door. The portrait on the wall was of Kaiser Wilhelm, not Franz Joseph, but in other respcts the place differed little from the Viennese coffee houses so dear to Carl's heart. A pianist was playing softly, and the waiter brought a morning paper to Carl's table unasked.

Carl sat over a cup of coffee for four hours. He read every newspaper to hand. He even engrossed himself in political trivialities rather than have to think about the match. To his chagrin, however, he came across an article on the world chess championship in every paper. One of them – the only one he didn't skip – was by Lasker himself. The world champion, whose fighting spirit was unequalled by any player alive, sounded surprisingly dispirited. He expected the final game to be a hard one and looked forward to it with scant confidence. Herr Haffner, he wrote, was second to none in his ability to elude a challenge and carried his safety-first play to extremes by entrenching himself.

Carl was rather hurt by these remarks. He laid the newspapers aside, puffed at his cigar, and surveyed the room. Eventually, he managed to set his thoughts adrift. He sat there, drinking coffee and smoking, until he felt easier in his mind.

His pangs of hunger became too much for him by early afternoon, but he shrank from taking advantage of the free lunch available at his hotel. He found a cheap restaurant and treated himself to a meal there. Afterwards, instead of returning to his analyses, he decided to go for a walk. The winter had veiled Berlin in fresh clouds during the previous night. Carl tramped the streets, hugging himself for warmth and ducking his head to shield his face from the bitter wind.

The world championship . . . It wasn't that he didn't value the title, but the burdens associated with that rank in the chess hierarchy filled him with trepidation. Not only because of the hungry challengers he would have to face, foremost among them the dreaded Lasker, but also because his obligations towards patrons, organizers and other masters – towards every chess enthusiast in the world, in a sense – would be overwhelmingly great. The world champion was an example to thousands. He was simultaneously revered and hunted. His

opinion counted. Every word he wrote was perused with care. In every tournament he was the measure of all things. His victories were taken for granted, his defeats were humiliations. The world champion had to prove himself
again and again.

That was precisely what lay in store for him – it came to him at that moment. There, in a chestnut-bordered avenue patrolled by old folk walking their dogs, he was assailed by the horrific realization that Lasker could not defeat him. The German's armoury contained no weapons capable of coping with his style of play. The tenth game, too, would end in a draw. His name would go down in the annals as the third world chess champion.

Carl was lost. He usually retained a mental image of every intersection and had never before gone astray in any city in the world. He tried to remember the way back, but in vain. He had to ask for directions.

On reaching the Hotel Kaiser he felt like having another coffee. By chance, he decided on the establishment where Fähndrich had sought Dutch courage the day before. The landlord recognized Carl's Austrian accent. He brought him a glass of schnapps on the side, winking as he did so. Carl, who could not remember ordering it, called the man over.

"Don't worry, it's on the house."

Carl said he never drank spirits. The landlord was undiscouraged. He gave Carl an impudent grin and winked at him so incessantly that Carl was afraid he'd fallen into the clutches of a madman. Finally, when the man started to sing the praises of his Austrian customers to the people at a neighbouring table, Carl picked up his jacket and hurried out.

*

Horak had invited Carl to a game of tarot that evening. They met in the hotel's smoking room, where the delegation from the Vienna Chess Club had taken up its quarters. The assistant secretaries were busy cutting out newspaper articles. Carl played with Horak, Wolf and Fähndrich. The latter was so dreadfully pale that even Carl noticed. "Feeling unwell, Fähndrich?" Horak asked curtly. "Shame on you! What have you been up to *this* time?"

Fähndrich seemed to shrink still further into his chair. Silent and submissive, he had been tormented all day long by the feeling that he was the most depraved individual on earth for having left his charge in the lurch. He dared not look anyone in the eye.

The foursome played like surgeons trying to banish the prospect of a dangerous operation. They spoke not a word more than necessary, had no taste for the customary comments and quotations, could not keep their minds on the game. The most abysmal mistakes went unpunished. Carl stared at his hand, but his thoughts were of Lasker, Lina, and the gold watch.

Anna came storming into the room, cheeks flushed with the cold, overcoat flapping behind her. Carl, who was happy to be wrested from his dire imaginings, welcomed her warmly and offered her a chair.

Horak rubbed his eyes. "It's getting late," he growled. "Let's call it a day."

It wasn't even nine. Carl was surprised but said nothing. They settled up. Horak and Wolf silently squeezed Carl's shoulder and took their leave. Fähndrich, too ashamed of himself to urge Carl to go to bed, slunk off with an anguished look on his face.

"I've driven them away," said Anna. "I'll tell you why another time."

Heedless of the other occupants of the smoking room, she proceeded, very softly, to sing Carl a Russian song. The words meant nothing to him. He smoked half a cigar with his head bowed, embarrassed by the glances of the hotel guests at the next table, and was relieved when Anna's song came to an end.

"It's about a little boy," she translated. "He has been given some bad marks at school and is afraid his stern father will beat him. On the way home he lies down in the shade of a beech tree. 'If only I'd got that thrashing over,' he thinks, and he recites a heartfelt prayer. A fairy appears. She gives the boy a ball of magic twine. 'Give it a tug,' she tells him, 'and time will pass. Take care, though. Don't tug too hard, and think carefully first.'

"The fairy vanishes. The boy, who's overjoyed, gives the twine a tug right away. In a flash he's six months older. He has grown a little, and his teeth are longer than they were. He thanks heaven he was spared the beating from his father.

"After that he uses the twine on numerous occasions – before going to the dentist, before sitting examinations, even before captaining his team in an important football match. Later on, before many a hard day's work or when he's sick, or when his wife is angry with him, or when his children keep him awake at night with their crying. One day, he happens to pass the beech tree where he was given the ball of twine so many years ago. By now his hair is white. He's eighty years old and has lived through only twenty of them. Guiltily, he thinks back on his life. He begins to weep and regrets that he ever tugged at the twine at all. The fairy reappears and takes it from him. The old man cries himself to sleep. He wakes to find himself the little boy who was scared of his father. He blithely runs home and takes his beating like a man."

"A nice story," said Carl. "But no, I don't need any ball of twine. My problem is quite different. I'm not afraid of losing the game tomorrow. I'm afraid of having to win it."

He shook off the diffidence that usually constrained him. He simply had to tell someone about the thought that had been plaguing him all day long. He would have to win the last game, he repeated.

"Why? A draw would do."

"No, it wouldn't. That's just it. A draw would be enough to win me the world championship, but not enough to make me a true world champion."

He spoke of his undeserved win in the fifth game. No honourable world champion could base his title on so fortuitous a victory. He would have to prove himself the stronger by winning the tenth game. He would have to deviate from his previous style of play and aim to win. He would have to attack, not entrench himself.

"I'm not qualified to give an opinion, I know too little about chess," Anna said. "All the same, might not that policy cost you dear? I'm told it doesn't suit you to play an attacking game."

"I haven't often tried," Carl replied. "It's quite possible, but what else can I do? I'm Lasker-proof, the way I've played till now. Strange as it may seem, he's incapable of beating me." He shrugged and gave a rather forlorn little chuckle. "I honestly wouldn't deserve the title after another draw. That's why I'll have to play for a decision – that's why I must try to win."

Did he think he was talking sense, Anna asked provocatively. She got no answer. Carl's attention was focused on a figure in a black tailcoat. A lean, angular man of melancholy mien, he went over to the piano and bowed. Carl, who knew the cheerful piece he proceeded to play, listened spellbound. Anna hummed the melody. Carl's excited reflections on the world championship were challenged, and eventually defeated, by the music. He and Anna said nothing until the piece came to an end. Then she stood up. Carl politely followed suit.

"All the best," she said. "Whom the gods would destroy they first make mad . . ."

Carl failed to grasp the significance of that quotation. It did not come from any of the ten literary classics he had read, but he responded with a friendly, understanding smile. Having escorted Anna to the door and expressed his thanks for her company, he hurried back to his chair. Although he was so tired he could scarcely keep his eyes open, and although he should have been preparing his opening for the morrow, he could not bring himself to leave. The pianist was no virtuoso, but he was a competent performer whose music conjured up memories of Carl's happiest hours.

The smoking room closed at one in the morning. The gaunt pianist with the melancholy eyes had completely banished Carl's sense of responsibility. He requested, nay begged, an encore, which the pianist granted him. Before going, he slipped some money into the man's hand.

It was around half-past two when Carl pushed open the door of his hotel room. Ignoring the chessboard, he got undressed like a man in a drunken stupor and crept beneath the bedclothes.

In utter despair after the ninth game, Lasker had asked Martha, the woman he had worshipped for years, to come to the Hôtel de Rome and lend him moral support during the final game. She sent word that she could not be of help: her husband had just died, and she was mourning him at home. For all his level-headedness, Lasker was not entirely devoid of superstition. He had been hoping that Martha's presence, which had served him well against Tarrasch, would change his luck. Now he would have to solve the Haffner problem on his own.

He did not touch the analysis board on the eve of the tenth game. Haffner was his superior as an opening theorist, and that superiority could not be eliminated in a few hours. Lasker worked out a plan of campaign in his head. Given the cautious way in which Haffner could be expected to respond, he decided to opt for an opening that would secure him a slight but lasting advantage. He might then, in the course of a long game, be able to force his opponent into making a crucial blunder.

Having completed his preparations, Lasker went fishing. Thereafter he played cards with his brother Berthold, dined with him at a fashionable restaurant, and treated himself to an expensive cigar. He retired to bed early. Although his hands were trembling when he awoke on the morning of the decider, he was dominated by a single, fixed idea: he wanted to win this final game more than anything else in the world.

He took care to turn up first as usual. Stationing himself on the platform with the arbiter beside him, he waited with head erect for Haffner to appear.

As in life, so in chess: you cannot attack until your opponent has handed you the requisite weapons.

Anna stood beside the refreshment tables, keenly observing the people who were surging into the already overcrowded room. Someone put his hands over her eyes from behind. She turned to find herself looking into Georg Hummel's fleshy

[148]

face. Rothschild and President Mandl, who were just to his rear, nodded to her. With a delighted exclamation, she threw her arms around Hummel's neck.

Hummel had found it intolerable to sit around in Vienna and wait for the moves to be wired to him. Eager to be present when a Viennese became world champion, he had cast aspersions on his editors' intelligence and put them off until after the match. He wasn't running much of a risk because his potent pen was indispensable to them. Baron von Rothschild had needed little persuading to accompany him, though Mandl had played hard to get.

Hummel had a batch of newspapers under his arm. He indicated the edition containing the piece on Berlin's night life and nipped the air with thumb and forefinger in confirmation that Anna had done an excellent job. Then he jabbed a finger at Horak, who was sipping a glass of port not far away. With a grin and a wink for Anna's benefit, he pushed his way through the crowd and slapped Horak on the shoulder from behind with the rolled-up newspaper.

"Here, you rascal," Anna heard him say, "I've got something for you. Fine things I've been reading about you!"

The rest of the conversation was drowned by applause. Craning her neck, Anna saw Fähndrich carving out Carl's route to the platform with a pair of ruthless elbows. There was much shoving and jostling. Here and there, chairs toppled over and glasses fell to the floor and smashed. Anna spilt her radish juice. The chess masters were rather restrained, but the ordinary spectators clapped and yelled and behaved with such wild glee that Anna abandoned all her own inhibitions. Hurling her glass at the floor, she squealed and shouted and screeched until she ran out of breath. This she did for fun, not for fear of the frenzied throng around her. She simply felt like it.

The mood of unbridled excitement was such that Dr Lewitt could not refrain from delivering a speech. He did the two principals no great favour by expatiating on the course of the match to date and recapitulating the position in which they found themselves at the start of the tenth game. Lasker subjected Carl to a self-confident stare, though his dearest wish was to get the game over and done with. Carl shuffled from foot to foot. He was dying to go to the lavatory, but was too embarrassed, with everyone watching, to sneak off to the clearly marked door. He was cold, too. He wiped the sweat from his brow with clammy hands, feeling as if he had a temperature.

For form's sake, the arbiter proceeded to read out the conditions under which the game would be played. Carl forgot his embarrassment. Looking neither to left nor right, he made a dash for the lavatory. His bowels voided water. Trembling all over, he hurried back to the platform and mounted it like a condemned man. Nothing could be heard but the ticking of the chess clock.

Lasker who was White, had already moved. He looked at Carl intently. With a hoarse sigh, Carl sat down, shook hands, and made his answering move. His bowels resumed their protests so violently that he hurried off to the lavatory without waiting for Lasker's response. It was occupied. He returned to the board, answered Lasker's second move without sitting down, and vanished through the door with the sign on it.

"He seems unwell," Anna whispered.

"He's scared stiff," growled Hummel. "Don't worry, it happens."

After the fifth move it was Carl's bladder, which he had only just emptied, that drove him from the table. His excretory organs gave him no trouble thereafter, but he still felt cold. He chafed his hands and arms, stood up and walked around, but to no avail. He drank a glass of red wine to stimulate his circulation.

The hall was less crowded now, many of the masters having withdrawn to adjacent rooms equipped with demonstration boards, where they discussed the game in animated tones. Messengers kept them up to date. Contrary to everyone's expectations, Carl had opted for a very demanding opening that gave promise of a lively game. Opinions were exchanged on the subject of his motives.

Hummel was standing, arms folded, in a corner from which he could survey the entire hall. He remained rooted to the spot, looking like a guard or policeman poised to intervene at any moment. He was not, in fact, perturbed by the course of the game, which he followed by means of sidelong glances at a demonstration board. He pictured Lasker and Haffner as two people confronting each other with a massive boulder between them and a team of fifty strong men at their backs. The teams consisted of each player's individual, personified strengths. Lasker's team pushed the boulder towards Haffner with all its might; Haffner's strained in the opposite direction. Lasker had already lost his footing once and ended up beneath the boulder. If he did not look out, he would suffer the same fate today. The most the German could do against Haffner was draw; Hummel had known that before the match began, but no one had believed him. Now they were all standing there with their mouths open, unable to fathom the sensational turn of events.

Hummel's thoughts filled him with such satisfaction that he giggled like a drunk whenever a move was effected on the platform. He became aware of this himself, after a while, and asked Anna if she knew where he could get a brandy. By the time Carl's tenth move had caused a stir, he was chewing on a Virginia cigar at the refreshment stand and rejoicing at the glow in his stomach.

In the adjoining rooms, everyone was shouting at once. Master Lipke, who was not averse to histrionics, exclaimed, "That's the most aggressive move Haffner has ever made!" Although this was an exaggeration, all the masters wondered how Haffner had summoned up the courage. All he needed was a draw, yet he was now playing an extremely risky game. His move was positionally sound and strong, but no one could have predicted it.

Lasker, who had gone off to get himself a drink, returned to the table with his usual upright stance. He saw Haffner's move and felt himself go hot. It was a while before he put his glass down and, never taking his eyes from the board, slowly resumed his seat. The game was still in the balance, at least. Lasker had no qualms in that respect, in fact he should really have been exultant: the Viennese was venturing out of his burrow for the very first time. But he found this so surprising that it had an unpleasant effect on him – indeed, it shook his composure a little. He had been fully prepared to besiege a fortress for hours on end, and now his opponent was sallying forth to meet him halfway.

Lasker ran his fingers through his hair. He raised his glass and put it down again, rested his chin first on one hand, then on the other.

Anna's eyes were watering. Everyone in sight was smoking a cigar or cigarette. Putting away the notebook in which she recorded her impressions, she went out into the street. The fresh air revived her. But, although it did her good to pace up and down in the snow, she could not bring herself to linger outside the hotel for long. It was not her eagerness to know the outcome of the contest that drove her back into the stuffy hall. She studied the spectators' faces with positively voyeuristic avidity. To those gathered round it, the board between the two men on the platform was the world's focal point. The eyes of many of the chess masters in the room were ablaze with quasi-religious fanaticism.

"It's a game," thought Anna. "When all is said and done, it's just a game. There's no divine message in a game of chess. I don't understand these people."

Carl became aware that he stank. His shirt was glued to his body with cold sweat. It was an intense, acrid smell, but he promptly banished it from his mind.

Horak was leaning against the wall with his arms folded. He had read Anna's article and handed it to Wolf without a word. He followed the game with an impassive air, chewing his moustache whenever he thought of the article. Now and then he gave a nervous laugh.

Fähndrich stared at the dirty floor and prayed.

Hummel was drinking brandy. He glanced at the demonstration board less often now.

The masters in the adjacent rooms had stopped arguing. All were concentrating on the game in silence, unwilling to be distracted from it by further talk. A waiter was circulating with a tray, and the clink of the glasses on it could be clearly heard.

The twelfth move. The fourteenth . . . A minor error on Lasker's part. His fifteenth move in response to Haffner's clever riposte . . . Another slip by the world champion.

Hummel didn't trouble to study the position in detail, an overall view was enough. This was no typical Haffner position.

Why was the idiot getting involved in such a game? Why was he pushing the boulder in Lasker's direction instead of simply spreading his legs and bracing himself against it?

Hummel invited Anna to have a brandy with him. Emptying his pockets, he built himself a nest on the refreshment stand with cigars, matches, grubby memorandum slips, writing materials, newspapers and nail files. He did not intend to move for some time.

The only person present to display no outward interest in the game was Dr Lewitt, who was paying court to Baron von Rothschild. He personally plied the distinguished guest with drinks and caviar rolls. He strove to entertain him with intelligent conversation. He discoursed on the history of chess, drew certain conclusions from it in respect of the Triple Alliance between Austria-Hungary, Germany and Italy, and, in an undertone, disclosed his opinion of the latest Balkan crisis. He gave Rothschild no peace until the latter brusquely remarked that he had come to Berlin to watch a game of chess and could dispense with Lewitt's learned dissertations. Unless Lewitt could restrain himself, he would see him after the game.

Dr Lewitt walked off shaking his head, appalled by the realization that Europe's foremost chess patron was an unrefined boor.

The twentieth move. The twenty-second, the twenty-fifth . . . Lasker captured one of his opponent's pawns.

Hummel left his improvised living-room table and went to fetch Fähndrich, who was still kneeling in a corner. They paused for a look at the demonstration board on their way back to the refreshment stand.

Hummel studied the current position. Stepping back, he shut one eye and spent ten minutes assessing the players' relative advantages and disadvantages. A smile dawned on his face. He glanced at Fähndrich, whose eyes were shining, then clapped his hands and laughed aloud. His immediate neighbours put fingers to lips and glared reprovingly.

Lasker's clock was ticking. Carl wasn't seated at the board. He had left the table and was chatting with Horak.

Hummel draped his arm round Fähndrich's shoulders and led him off to the refreshment stand, where they toasted the royal game in brandy.

The adjournment. Carl slipped away without a word. The masters came streaming out of the side rooms and into the main hall. Waiters were bombarded with orders from all quarters. Hummel's deep voice boomed out at the refreshment stand. Everyone milled around. The masters gesticulated excitedly as they underlined the sensational turn the game had taken. In Carl's camp, which the world's leading masters had now joined, his chances of winning were put at sixty or seventy per cent.

Baron von Rothschild invited the Viennese delegates to dine at one of the finest restaurants in the city. Carl conveyed his excuses via Fähndrich, saying that he still had some analysing to do and could not, therefore, join them. Mandl was all for talking Carl into it, but Hummel restrained him. "Let him rest. After all, he'll be world champion by this time tomorrow."

This conversation took place in the lobby of the Hotel Kaiser, just as they were preparing to leave. Hummel clapped a hand to his brow. "I've forgotten something," he exclaimed. "Go ahead, I'll catch you up outside."

As quickly as his corpulent frame permitted, Hummel hurried upstairs to the floor on which Carl's room was situated. Rather diffidently, he knocked on the door. When there was no sound of movement inside, he produced some press cuttings from his pocket. Sinking to his knees with a groan, he slid the cuttings under the door. Then he straightened up, smoothed his trousers, and thundered downstairs again.

The newspaper articles, most of which were by Hummel himself, extolled the challenger's play and predicted that he would win the match. They were intended to provide Carl with some pleasant bedtime reading.

Fähndrich woke Carl promptly. On opening the door to him, Carl felt the press cuttings rustle underfoot. Having picked them up and glanced at the headlines, he deposited them on his bed without heeding them further.

After breakfast, Carl consented to drink half a glass of champagne with Fähndrich, who gave him a hilarious account of last night's festivities. His description of Hummel singing audacious revolutionary songs made Carl slap his thigh with mirth. They almost forgot the time, they became so absorbed in their conversation. Their state of mind was that of people who had not slept for two days but were into their second wind.

Lasker was standing beside the board when Carl mounted the platform. A photographer took some pictures. The arbiter made his usual preliminary announcement and started the clock. Hummel, like the universally popular figure he was, held court at the refreshment stand.

For the first few minutes of the game, Carl was once more plagued by indigestion. Hummel delivered a coarse but jocular comment on his toings and froings between the lavatory and the platform. Rebuked by some spectators who were unacquainted with him, he acknowledged their reprimand with a bow and a military salute. After this, he did not stray far from the refreshment stand. When in the mood, Hummel could be highly entertaining. He was rapidly approaching that condition, and they could not afford to miss a word.

Moves thirty-one, thirty-two, thirty-three . . . Haffner was playing a strong, logical game. An icy wind was whistling round Lasker's king, which had remained in the centre.

Rothschild went over to the photographer. "Do me a favour, will you? Take some pictures of those two gentlemen." He indicated Mandl and Dr Lewitt. "But please don't let them know you're doing it for me."

The photographer took the banknote Rothschild slipped into his hand. With a cigarette dangling casually from the corner of his mouth, he went to get his camera.

Rothschild informed Hummel in a whisper of his request to the photographer. Hummel raised a delighted eyebrow. Together, they watched the photographer parlaying with his victims. Lewitt and Mandl, having initially refused, let him talk them round. At the refreshment stand, Hummel accompanied their preparations for the photographs with some comic mime. He struck a pose, spat on his hands and slicked his hair down. Just as he was proudly presenting his profile to Rothschild, Fähndrich tugged at his sleeve. Hummel put a finger to his lips and rolled his eyes.

"Stop that tomfoolery and come with me!" Fähndrich hissed. He towed Hummel over to the demonstration board.

Lasker had just completed his thirty-fourth move. Hummel immersed himself in the position. Fähndrich, whose ears had taken on a crimson tinge, closely observed Hummel's every change of expression.

Before Hummel could pass judgement on the position, Carl made his answering move. A secretary reproduced it on the demonstration board. Hummel gasped like a stranded fish and thrust Fähndrich into an adjoining room. The masters assembled there laughed and shook their heads.

"Is he mad?" hissed Hummel. "What's he doing? Why didn't he centralize his knight?"

"Precisely!" Fähndrich exclaimed. "He really seems determined to win at all costs."

Hummel took soundings among the other masters. Most of them shared his opinion. By centralizing his knight, Haffner could have secured a safe advantage and forced a comfortable draw, if nothing more. The move he had chosen was even stronger, viewed objectively, but it was an attacking move that precluded a draw. There was no doubt about it, someone must have doctored Haffner's coffee. The Viennese challenger had lost his wits: he was playing to win.

Hummel waddled through the side rooms. The brandy he had drunk was no help to him now. He mopped his sweating brow with a rather dirty handkerchief. His hands were trembling so badly, he almost failed to light a cigar. Unwilling to re-enter the match room, he persuaded Fähndrich to keep him supplied with brandy. On returning from one of these errands, Fähndrich reported in a quavering voice that Carl was strolling around the room, lightheartedly chatting with friends. Hummel tapped his forehead and almost burst into tears with agitation.

Lasker played his thirty-fifth move. A messenger hurried through the rooms and reproduced it on all the demonstration boards. Most of the masters nodded contentedly and rubbed their hands. It had developed into the most exciting game of the series by far – wild, complex, and almost reminiscent in style of the old Romantics.

Carl had been pondering his response for eleven minutes. No

one was worried by this, given all the time he had accumulated.

When he still had not moved after eighteen minutes, Hummel reluctantly submitted himself to the ordeal of studying the position closely.

Carl was not pondering his move, he was experiencing a sense of déjà-vu. He had once been in a similar position. He could not remember where or when, but it must have been a very long time ago. Whom had he been playing?

Thirty-two minutes . . . Hummel nudged Fähndrich and pointed to the demonstration board. "Am I hallucinating?" he asked, his eyes shining. "Or do you see what I see?"

Carl remembered who his opponent had been and could not help laughing. He addressed himself to the game once more.

Forty-four minutes . . . Hummel was holding Fähndrich's hand. The masters in front of the demonstration boards had only now grasped Haffner's underlying design. The challenger had outplayed the world champion in a positively brilliant fashion. If Haffner moved his rook to d8, Lasker's position would be in ruins and he might as well resign at once. There would be no escape.

Fifty-one minutes. Fifty-two . . . Carl wavered between two alternatives. If he moved his rook to d8, the game would be over in minutes and he would have scored an attractive victory. If he sacrificed the exchange with the rook to f4, on the other hand, he would not only have a chance of winning: he might be able to present the chess world with a jewel of a game – a game to be treasured for evermore. The first alternative was safe, the second exceedingly risky.

Carl had now been considering his move for fifty-eight minutes. He was muttering unintelligibly to himself, Anna noticed. His cheeks were pale, his fingers toyed with the captured pieces beside the board. Lasker sat hunched in his chair, his head cupped in his hands. His face was invisible. He seemed to have forgotten about the cigar between his fingers. The ash broke off, rolled over the back of his hand, and landed on the board. Carl said "Excuse me" and blew it away. Lasker didn't stir.

Sixty-four minutes . . . "What's he waiting for?" Hummel exclaimed.

Carl captured the pawn on f4. He stood up, rubbing his eyes, and strolled over to Wolf.

"Why not the rook to d8?" Wolf whispered excitedly.

Carl shrugged. "A matter of taste."

Carl asked Anna how she could endure to watch a game of chess for hours without once sitting down. She laughed. "Have you any idea how many hours I've had to pose for a painter without moving?"

Carl went over to the refreshment stand. He looked for Hummel but failed to see him. Nearby, Mandl and Dr Lewitt were debating which newspapers would carry their photograph. Carl drank a glass of milk. No one ventured to speak to him for fear of spoiling his concentration, though he would, in fact, have welcomed a talk with someone. He resumed his place at the board and re-immersed himself in the position.

Hummel moved his chair into a corner from which the demonstration board was invisible. Fähndrich brought him a glass of brandy. Hummel waved it away. The thought of drinking it turned his stomach.

The thirty-seventh move, the thirty-eighth . . . Hummel counted the spots on his trousers. Fähndrich reported that Carl had already been pondering his thirty-ninth move for twenty minutes.

"How's it going?" Hummel asked feebly.

"I'm not sure. Mieses and Tartakower think he can force a draw. In my opinion, it may already be impossible."

Hummel jumped up. He rudely thrust aside the masters who were debating in front of the board.

Carl had realized that his capturing of the pawn at f4 was a miscalculation. Once again, two choices presented themselves. He could secure a draw by giving check with his queen on h4 and bringing the game to a favourable conclusion. If he moved the queen to h1, on the other hand, he would be maintaining his attack. Strictly speaking, this was his one remaining way of winning the game. Lasker would, however, have to oblige him by making a slip. If he didn't, he might well beat off the attack and win.

Fähndrich conceded that he had been wrong. The masters in the side rooms unanimously agreed that the queen's move to h4 would force a draw. Anything else would be a reckless invitation to disaster.

The messenger came in. Hummel shut his eyes, heard his neighbours' heavy breathing. Cries rang out. Someone pounded a table with his fist. Hummel squinted at the board. The queen was on h1, not h4.

Fähndrich mimed a hanged man. Hummel tottered out into the playing hall and asked for a glass of water at the refreshment stand. Anna had to light his cigar for him.

"Things aren't looking too good, I'm told."

"He's as good as dead, but he doesn't realize it. Or does he? It makes no difference." Hummel muttered the words without looking at Anna. "What on earth am I doing here?"

He relinquished his place at the refreshment stand and left the hotel without a good-bye to anyone.

Carl's attack ground to a halt, as the kibitzers had predicted.

The game was adjourned until next morning. Horak and a dozen or more masters converged on Carl. "What got into you?" one of them demanded. "You could have had it all – a win, a draw, whichever you wanted!" Other voices chimed in. "He cogitated for an hour and played like a child! The fool had victory in his grasp!"

"Don't tell me you failed to spot the rook to d8," Horak said darkly. "Any novice can think three moves ahead."

"The rook to d8? I overlooked that. Excuse me, I need some fresh air."

They tried to detain him, but he threw up his arms in entreaty and dashed out of the hotel. He ran until the Hotel Kaiser came into view. Locking his door, he threw himself down on the bed without even taking his shoes off. His lungs hurt as if they were being rent asunder, his heartbeat threatened to choke him.

He recovered his breath a little. Then he drew the curtains so as not to be distracted from his labours by the sunlight or the sight of the impressive buildings across the street. He analysed the game for eleven hours without a break, pausing only to consume one of his favourite Kaiserschmarren, which Fähndrich had got the hotel chef to make him.

Late that night he went to bed. He realized that his opponent's material advantage was decisive. Unless Lasker blundered, the game was lost.

At the resumption, the players' state of mind was obvious. Carl's pallid face twitched incessantly. He smoked two cigars at once without realizing it, singed his hair by drawing the back of his hand across his brow from time to time, and studiously avoided looking at his opponent.

Whenever Lasker was seated at the board, waiting for Carl to move, he stared at him. The world champion looked rested.

He puffed at his cigar with relish and took little time over his moves. Bright-eyed, he strolled round the room and chatted with friends in a relaxed manner.

All the masters in the building knew that the outcome of the game was a foregone conclusion. Their hearts went out to Carl as he sat on the platform in solitary state, looking for a non-existent way out of his predicament. Hummel alone remained defiant. "There isn't a tougher or more skilful defensive player in the world," he said with a sour smile. "Wait and see. Haffner has held all kinds of positions in his time."

After sixty moves Carl's position was so hopeless that he considered resigning. "So I'm losing," he thought. "Lina loves me, that's the main thing."

Then he thought of the gold watch and pulled himself together again. But, no matter what artifices he employed, Lasker relentlessly pursued the right course. On the third day of the tenth game, the world champion played like a true world champion at last. He left his opponent no chance.

Carl played the last few moves purely as a means of preparing himself inwardly for defeat. He thought of enjoyable games of tarot, of reading newspapers in coffee houses, of going for walks, of a comfortable existence unburdened by the world championship. He recalled the scent of lavender in Lina's apartment, their meals together, her piano recitals. He had Lina; he needed no world title.

Hummel and Fähndrich learned of Haffner's resignation outside the Hôtel de France. Rather than await the end in the crowded match room, they walked with heads bowed and dragging footsteps to the next crossroads and back. Horak emerged into the street and gestured from afar to convey that it was all over. Hummel came to a halt. He spat and uttered an oath. Fähndrich gripped him by the arm. "Now let's go in and congratulate our man," he said. "In spite of everything."

The closing ceremony was scheduled to take place two hours after the last game. In the interim, word was sent to those local dignitaries who wished to attend the prize-giving.

Everyone marvelled at the loser's composure. Carl strolled around looking as cheerful as if he had won. He readily consented to be photographed with Lasker, and many people, if asked to identify the victor by his demeanour, would have picked the wrong man. Lasker's acknowledgement of the congratulations he received was restrained. For one thing, this had been his sixth world championship, so he was no stranger to the sensation of victory. For another, his pleasure was muted by an awareness of how close he had come, this time, to defeat.

The Viennese delegates hovered at the refreshment stand, looking disconsolate. The only exception was Rothschild, who was joking with an honorary consul in an effort to seem impartial. Fähndrich was in the worst state of all. Supporting himself with one arm draped round Hummel's shoulders, he wept unashamedly as he watched the goings-on in the room. Hummel could not console him. He chewed his Virginia cigar and mopped his eyes from time to time.

Carl came over to them with his arms flung wide. "My dear Fähndrich, what's the matter? Did we lose? No! Well, then! Nothing's wrong – nothing!"

Fähndrich could not speak. His lips were trembling. "I know one thing," Hummel snarled. "There'll be a next time. I will see thee at Philippi, Herr Lasker!"

His pince-nez had fallen off and were dangling by their ribbon. He jammed them on his nose and turned away. Carl slowly lowered his arms, abruptly conscious of what he had done to his chess friends. He had forgotten his duty towards the people who had supported him. His composure vanished.

"I notice that everyone apart from your Viennese companions is avoiding you," said Anna. "Why do you think that is?"

Carl shook his head. "I don't know. They're probably wondering what to say to me."

"What *should* they say to you? What should *I* say to you, for that matter? Which are in order at such a moment, condolences or congratulations?"

Carl, who had laughed at the word "condolences", looked thoughtful.

"You don't seem very depressed," Anna went on. "Not, at any rate, like someone whose dearest hopes have been dashed. So tell me, how should I treat you now? Rather more gingerly than usual – like an invalid, say – or like an adventurer who has returned home safe and sound?"

Dr Lewitt clapped his hands to signify that the closing ceremony was about to begin. The playing area had been converted into a speaker's platform and the room provided with additional rows of chairs.

Anna pushed Carl ahead of her and prevailed on him to sit down in the front row. The other Viennese masters were loath to leave the refreshment stand, but she plied them with heartening words and led them over to the chairs one by one. Fähndrich she gestured into the seat beside Carl. She herself sat down in the row immediately behind them.

Dr Lewitt welcomed the dignitaries present and thanked all those who had helped run the event so smoothly. He paid special tribute to the efforts of the president of the Vienna Chess Club, under whose aegis the first half of the contest had been held in such a careful and responsible manner. Mandl, in his turn, uttered a few words of praise for the work of his Berlin friends. Tickled by the sight of the two proud presidents on the podium, Hummel recovered his sense of humour. He rose to his feet and gained the twin officials a standing ovation by bellowing *"Bravi! Bravi! Bravissimi!"*

Unruffled by this patently exaggerated mark of homage, Dr Lewitt took the floor once more. He thanked the organizers for having granted the world the pleasure of witnessing chess played at the highest level. Then he gave a résumé of the contest.

"This duel proved more exciting than any stage play," his speech concluded. "Ultimately, however, the old world champion remained victorious – old, of course, in the sense of tried and tested, for he's ardently youthful in spirit. You will recall that Mr Hugo Jackson has donated a gold watch to be awarded to the winner of the contest. This watch, a superb piece of craftsmanship, I now present to the esteemed Dr Lasker."

"This is a vile injustice!" shouted someone in the front row. No one could believe, at first, that it was meek Carl Haffner who had sprung to his feet and was shaking his fist at the platform.

"Unfair and unjust!" yelled Carl. "There was neither a winner nor a loser in this match. Dr Lasker is still world champion, yes, but he failed to clinch the match in his favour. This award is outrageous, scandalous! I strongly protest! I shall take no further part in this ceremony!"

Carl ran from the room. Fähndrich, appalled, could not restrain him. One or two people stood up. Startled exclamations rang out. Fähndrich, Horak and Wolf followed their indignant friend out into the street. Lasker donned a calm and detached expression. Lewitt and Mandl eyed each other helplessly. A babble of voices filled the air, all of them discussing this latest sensation.

Fähndrich rejoined Hummel a few minutes later, looking pale. "He's absolutely furious," he reported. "I've never seen him in such a state – kicking the wall, yelling obscenities, cursing the organizers. He flatly refuses to come back, claims he's been cheated. He won't change his mind."

Hummel draped his coat round his shoulders and hurried out. He returned soon afterwards, shaking his head. "What's got into him?" he said to Anna. "He's behaving the way Janowski does when he loses a game. I'm surprised he isn't foaming at the mouth!"

He blew on his hands. "Very well, let's cut the rest of the proceedings and make ourselves scarce."

Anna had been too tactful to follow Carl out into the street, though she found his outburst most endearing. It showed that even he was not invariably submissive.

The two presidents went outside to calm Carl down. The hotel management trundled a piano into the hall, and the resident pianist entertained the assemblage for half an hour. The presidents' efforts eventually bore fruit. Carl followed them back into the hall two paces to their rear, head hanging, and resumed his seat without looking up. His expression was eloquent of his reluctance to attend the ceremony and his desire to get the whole thing over as quickly as possible.

The gold watch was duly presented to Lasker, who thanked the organizers for all their hard work. The whole of the closing ceremony was as frigid and formal as Lasker's speech. The world champion recalled the strength of his opponent's game, which had made him a dangerous adversary to the very last move. As for a return match, he would address that matter in a year or two.

By the time Dr Lewitt prepared to placate Carl by paying him a personal tribute, the challenger's seat was empty. He limited himself to a few brief closing remarks, reiterated that Dr Lasker had retained the world title, and declared the proceedings at an end. Some half-hearted applause, and the crowd quickly dispersed with a few perfunctory handshakes. Now that the atmosphere had been irretrievably soured, everyone was glad to leave it behind.

Little was said during the long train journey back to Vienna. Trivial remarks were exchanged. Nobody mentioned the match. The Viennese delegates sat in their compartments in a kind of daze. Fähndrich thought dismally of their mood on the way to Berlin, their dreams of a Viennese world champion.

The party broke up at the station. A handshake, a nod, and they went their separate ways without more ado.

||||||| REJECTION |||||||

Lina's apartment was not Carl's first port of call – his conscience was troubling him because of the gold watch – nor did he want to return to his lodgings. Instead, he paid his mother a visit. It was not until he had trudged down the steps to the basement that he realized how ill he felt.

His mother gave him a hug. "Well, did you win the world championship? Never mind, it doesn't matter."

She led him into the living room. He put his suitcase down.

"Heavens, what a picture of health you look!" Maria exclaimed. "Sunken cheeks, hollow eyes!"

Within minutes, Carl was tucked up in the bed he'd slept in as a boy. Although he was no giant, to say the least, its dimensions no longer fitted him. He had to dangle his feet over the end, not that this bothered him. He felt weak but safe and snug. His mother brought him some tea and slid a hot brick under the bedclothes.

Carl had shed fourteen pounds in the course of the championship. Maria said he looked like a consumptive. Disregarding all his protests, she kept him house-bound for several weeks and gave him two hot meals a day. At the beginning of the last week she permitted him to play a little chess. She dusted off his father's chessboard and, with a wry expression, deposited it on his bed.

It was the end of March by the time Maria allowed him out. The snow had melted long ago, and the streets were redolent of a mild spring. Carl was unworried by his failure to win the gold watch as he made his way to Zimmermanngasse. The closer he got to Lina's home, the faster he walked. He could already hear the piano as he climbed the stairs, a crudely executed scale that told him Lina was giving a lesson. He paused to catch his breath. The door was unlocked. He slipped off his shoes and straightened his tie, then stole into the music room. Lina was facing away from the door. He kissed the nape of her neck – kissed it quite without thinking, as if in a dream.

A press cutting dated 1919. Beneath the apt heading "Miscellaneous" are two items of chess news. The first concerns Emanuel Lasker.

"**World Champion's Lecture.** World Chess Champion Dr Lasker delivered a lecture at the Architektenhaus on his new philosophical treatise, *The Philosophy of the Unfinished.*"

There follow thirty lines devoted to the contents of Lasker's latest book, which was not yet on sale.

The full text of the second report:

"**Carl Haffner** †. Chess Master Carl Haffner died of pneumonia at a Budapest hospital on 27 December last. He was in his forty-eighth year."

Little remains to be added, except that the writer made two mistakes. Carl Haffner was forty-four, not forty-seven or forty-eight. Furthermore, while it is true that he was suffering from a lung complaint, he did not die of that or pneumonia. He starved to death.

The Viennese masters soon got over their disappointment at Haffner's last-minute failure to gain the world title. After a week's mourning, newspapers in nearly every European country published articles dealing with the world championship and paying tribute to Carl Haffner's sensational performance. Their gist was that Lasker had been extremely lucky to escape defeat, and that Haffner was his equal. The chess world now had two world champions. What was more, there must be a return match.

During this propaganda campaign, which was conducted in masterly fashion by Georg Hummel, Hamburg held a major tournament. Invitations were accepted by all the world's leading players except Lasker. The tournament was won by Carl Haffner. The ten games of the world championship had enhanced the Austrian's style. Although he remained the king of the drawn game, his play was more unpredictable, perceptive and elegant than before. Had anyone prophesied that summer that Hamburg would be Haffner's last great tournament victory, he would have been laughed to scorn.

Hummel sent challenge after challenge to Berlin. Lasker either failed to reply or wrote a few lines in which he regretfully pleaded professional engagements and put off the Viennese masters until the following year. In 1911 he did, in fact, find time for a world championship match against Janowski. The result – eight-nil to Lasker with three games drawn – surprised no one except the defeated challenger. Hummel passed some acid comments on this contest. It was common knowledge that Janowski enjoyed the backing of Nardus, the French chess patron, and could therefore put up a considerably bigger purse than Vienna, all the Rothschilds notwithstanding. Lasker was engaging in a farce for money's sake, Hummel wrote, instead of taking on the worthiest challenger. Thereafter, Lasker severed all contact with the Viennese masters.

Anna abandoned her investigation of the chess fraternity and Carl's character in particular. The actual nature of those who played chess defied her comprehension. She found the game too remote and esoteric. As an art form, it bore no relation to reality and was thus, strictly speaking, not an art form at all. As for Carl himself, Anna shrank from the effort it would cost her to explore him further.

They met again on only three occasions. The last time Anna bumped into him, Carl was strolling along one of the Prater's tree-lined walks with his sister, whom he introduced to her. Anna thought he looked happier than before. She had the impression that he wanted to tell her something but could not find the words. Years later, when she learned of his death, she recalled how he had stood facing her that day in the Prater: a nice little chess-player with an amiable expression – one for whom a chequered board harboured the world's greatest mysteries. All she remembered of his sister was her plain but pleasing style of dress.

"A good-looking woman," Lina remarked to Carl, when they had said good-bye to Anna and walked on.

"You think so? I don't know."

They were crossing a broad expanse of grass. "Carl," Lina said suddenly, "is she your sweetheart?"

"Of course not!" Carl exclaimed. "You're my sweetheart."

"You know what I mean. Is she or isn't she? Surely you can tell me?"

Carl came to a halt. "You're my sweetheart, Lina, you know that."

He clasped her to him. It was the first time he had kissed a woman on the lips. Lina freed herself, avoiding his eye. She looked rather upset, and that made him feel awkward in some strange way. They never mentioned the incident.

A few weeks later, Carl's mother gave up her lavatory attendant's job. She had saved some money and was now entitled to a small pension. Carl agreed to move with her to Brunn in Lower Austria. That year, 1912, he became sole editor of the *Deutsche Schachzeitung*. He also started work on a revised edition of Paul von Bilguer's *Handbuch des Schachspiels*, a monumental, thousand-page work on chess theory. These tasks he thought it would be easier to perform in the seclusion of Brunn. Once or twice a month he travelled to Vienna to visit the chess club or meet his friends for a hand of tarot. "Leave him be," said Hummel. "He won't be able to stand it in the wilds for long. He's a big-city flower – he'll soon be back."

Carl took part in the Baden tournament of 1914, but only in order to try out some gambit variations he was editing in the Bilguer. He did not lose a single one of the eighteen games in the tournament and gained third place. Hummel urged him to reappear on the international stage. Carl said he regretted his inability to grant Hummel's request, but he wanted to finish the Bilguer first. Hummel, who didn't give a fig for his objections, kept on at Carl until he consented at least to play in the Trebitsch tournament at Vienna. Carl won first prize, although he lost the last game. It was his second defeat in 104 games since Piešt'any in 1912.

For Carl, the First World War meant poverty and hardship. Few of the chess periodicals that employed him survived the first two years of the fighting. He finished work on the Bilguer in 1916, by which time he and his mother were not getting enough to eat. He moved back to Vienna so as not to be a burden on her, ostensibly because his presence there was necessitated by his participation in numerous tournaments.

He was lying: there weren't any tournaments in Vienna. The war had brought chess activity in Austria-Hungary to a standstill. Carl's only income derived from the occasional simultaneous displays arranged by chess enthusiasts. He refused to accept help from the Vienna Chess Club, which was still a wealthy institution, being unwilling to follow the example of Albin, who had allowed the club to feed and house him since the outbreak of war. For a while, he managed to hoodwink Georg Hummel with assurances that he was not in any kind of financial difficulty and had saved enough to weather the storm. When he became ever thinner and his appearances at the chess club ever rarer, however, Hummel grasped the truth. He consulted the club's treasurers, who offered Carl a monthly allowance. By now, every step he took made him dizzy and every breath he drew hurt his lungs, but he still found the energy to decline the club's help with thanks. Hummel thereupon created the post of club analyst. He hurried off to Carl's lodgings with a substantial advance on his first month's salary. Carl was undeceived. "I'm still recovering from the Bilguer," he said. "I don't want to do much analysing for a while."

Hummel could restrain himself no longer. He seized Carl by the collar and swore at him. Finally, in despair, he invited him to play a match. Carl declined that offer as well. He would play only if it had not been arranged especially for his benefit and would have taken place in any case.

"Others need the money just as much," he said quietly.

Hummel seriously considered getting Carl certified insane

and committed to a lunatic asylum, where the club could see to it that he was force-fed. He would have put this plan into effect, what is more, but he hadn't the time. Other chess masters were now in dire straits. They flocked to Vienna from all over the country, begging for help. Hummel robbed Peter to pay Paul, procured rail and ship tickets, purchased food coupons, rented lice-ridden lodgings, organized matches. He was too busy to traipse all the way across Vienna, corner a reluctant Carl Haffner, and entreat him to accept help. There were too many others waiting outside the door of the chess club.

In October 1918, a handful of patrons clubbed together to finance a small tournament in Berlin. They sent invitations to Lasker, Tarrasch, and Rubinstein. Then someone remembered the Austrian who had scored some notable successes before the war, and Carl was invited to become the fourth participant.

Lasker flinched when he shook hands with his old adversary. Carl's appearance was so horrific that the world champion averted his eyes. He had never seen a more emaciated man, not even in the most poverty-stricken districts of Berlin. It seemed incredible that he could still stay on his feet. His face was grey, the skin almost transparent, and his lips were bloodless. Everyone could tell that he was in pain. All in all, he looked like an ailing man of sixty.

But he did not play like one. He often had to rest during play, shut his eyes until he seemed to have dozed off, and needed more thinking time than in the old days. When he studied a position, however, colour came into his cheeks and his eyes lit up, and it was plain that he felt as well as circumstances permitted. His play had deteriorated, admittedly, but that was because of his physical condition. In one of his two games against Lasker he stood to win. He lost when exhaustion caused him to blunder after many hours at the board.

That was Carl's penultimate tournament. He came third.

On 11 December 1918, when he alighted from the train at Budapest, he had eaten no solid food for five whole days. Tamás Horváth, a representative from the Budapest Chess Club, was dismayed by his appearance. He took his guest's arm and conducted him to the station buffet. Attributing Carl's condition to the effects of some illness, he ordered him some tea and *barack*. Carl consented to take this medicine. He answered the Hungarian's questions in a hoarse, monosyllabic voice, almost in a whisper. Horváth accompanied him to his hotel and summoned a doctor. The doctor later informed the worried official that Herr Haffner had thanked him for coming but refused to be examined and assured him that he was feeling better.

Of the eight games Carl played at Budapest, he lost five and drew three. The organizers did not have enough funds to feed the participants, only to pay for their hotel rooms. The prize money was modest, too, but this was irrelevant to Carl because his placing was too low to merit a prize. When he set off for the station on 23 December, not a crumb of Hungarian food had passed his lips.

He was feeling tired and feverish. It was so cold that he scratched himself with a comb in an effort to boost his circulation and drew blood. He longed to see his mother, with whom he had promised to spend Christmas at Brunn. All he could think of was a night in the warm beside a decorated Christmas tree.

On the way to the ticket office he had to go to the lavatory. He left his bag in the booking hall. When he returned it had gone. It contained all his belongings: clothes, unfinished manuscripts, papers, and the money for the return fare, which he had put aside as usual.

The walk to the station had exhausted him. He took three times as long to get to the Budapest Chess Club, where he despairingly informed Horváth of his loss. He did not know what to do. He had no savings, even in Vienna, that he could send for.

Horváth reached an understanding with the members of the Budapest Chess Club, who jointly contributed enough to replace what the Austrian master had lost. Since it was obvious that he could not make the journey home in his debilitated condition, they paid for a hotel room as well.

Instead of spending Christmas Eve at Brunn, therefore, Carl spent it in a sparsely furnished room at the Hotel Balaton. Some tea and a meal were brought to his bedside, but he could no longer keep anything down. He didn't know how he made it to the lavatory each time, but he was thankful not to have soiled the bed or the floor.

On 27 December, Carl got ready to leave. His recurrent spells of dizziness were such that it took him nearly an hour to dress. He groped his way along step by step, leaning against the wall for support. In the street he collapsed and was taken to hospital, where a doctor sounded his chest. The diagnosis, as recorded in his medical notes by a nurse: "Pneumonia."

Carl remained unconscious for the last few hours. This spared him the sight of the overcrowded ward, the nurses stepping over makeshift beds to get from one patient to another, and the admonitory crucifix slumbering on the bare, whitewashed wall.

In May 1899, Carl took part in a local Viennese tournament. It was a minor event – little more than a training exercise. Carl had been playing less to win than for fun, and it became clear before the last round that he would have to win his game in order to clinch the tournament in his favour.

Carl's opponent in the last round was Joseph Schwarz, over sixty years old and a rather weak player. The game followed a predictable course. Carl easily gained an advantage. After twenty-five moves, Schwarz's position was precarious in the extreme.

Carl played his twenty-sixth move and rose to fetch himself a glass of water. Schwarz gestured to him to remain seated. Although puzzled, Carl complied. Schwarz made his answering move and fixed Carl with a watery blue eye. Then, after blowing his nose with great deliberation, he said, "Will you accept a draw, Herr Haffner?"

Carl gulped. He had not foreseen such a request. Most players would have been too proud to offer a draw in such a hopeless position. Carl muttered that he would have to think it over.

He did not at first consider the offer. Instead, he worked out a number of variations. Unless he made a mistake, his opponent was past saving.

The old man was watching him expectantly, he noticed. Getting up, he strolled over to the blackboard that bore the tournament table. His two nearest rivals had already won their games. This meant that, if he beat Schwarz, he would share first place with them; if he drew, he would come third. The table told him something else: a defeat against Carl would place Schwarz last of all, whereas a draw would promote him to second last.

Carl looked back at his opponent. Schwarz was fidgeting in his chair, fiddling with a button on his jacket, shuffling his feet. He reminded Carl a little of an excited youngster at his very first tournament.

Carl tried to recall what he knew of the old man. Schwarz's wife was dead, and he had no children. He hadn't been playing chess for long. He lived in modest lodgings in the suburbs and spent his time in cafés, waiting for someone to play chess with him and pass the time of day. Carl had occasionally caught sight of the old man in some coffee house, a solitary figure seated before a chessboard. He had a reputation for cussedness and did not appear to have many friends.

Carl came up behind Schwarz and studied the position once more. He could not help smiling at his opponent's naivety. He eyed his thin back, frayed collar and grimy cuffs, his sparse, wispy hair. All at once, he felt profoundly sorry for the old man. More than that, he felt drawn to him.

He sat down and shook hands with Schwarz to denote that he had accepted a draw. The old man vainly strove to conceal his elation. Carl signed the score sheet and paid respectful tribute to his opponent's play. The expression on Schwarz's face touched him.

Hummel came over to the table. "A draw?" he barked. "Are you drunk, man?"

"I'm tired," said Carl. "I can't concentrate today. Besides, this tournament doesn't matter overmuch."

Hummel remonstrated with Carl until he had to promise not to give any more points away, no matter what the occasion. Schwarz butted in. "What are you getting at?" he snapped at Hummel. "It's a dead draw! He can't touch me. If he played so, I'd reply so. I'd parry that move with my rook . . ."

Hummel, shaking his head, demonstrated why Schwarz would have been bound to lose, but the old man remained adamant. He dismissed the explanation. "A wholly justified draw,"he insisted. The bystanders chuckled at his vehemence.

Schwarz did not turn up for the prize-giving. He had won no prize, so Carl was the only one who noticed the absence of his grizzled head.

When the closing ceremony was over, Carl made his adieus and left. He walked to the Café Nagel, Schwarz's regular haunt, where he ordered a coffee and kept watch on the old man from behind a newspaper. Schwarz was going from table to table, beaming with delight and showing off the score sheet to his acquaintances. Carl watched this performance for a while. Then he finished his coffee and beckoned the waiter. In high spirits, he left the establishment before the old man could catch sight of him. It was a warm evening. The lamplighter had yet to go on his rounds. Cab horses were clip-clopping along the street. Carl lit a cigar.

Someone in the café, who had spotted him going out, turned to Schwarz and said, "He was here."

Schlechter, Karl, Austrian grandmaster, b. 1874, d. 1918; at the beginning of the twentieth century, one of the world's foremost players. In 1910 he drew a world championship match against Lasker, though Lasker retained the title. His best tournament results: Munich 1900, first equal with Pillsbury; Ostende 1906, first prize ahead of Maróczy and Rubinstein; Prague 1908, first equal with Duras; Hamburg 1910, first prize ahead of Duras. Schlechter was the strongest member of the Viennese chess school, with an outstanding knowledge of openings, a fine positional style, and a mode of play that was always geared to safety. During his career he played some 700 games, over fifty per cent of them drawn.

Lasker, Emanuel, world chess champion 1894–1921, b. 1868 at Berlinchen (Brandenberg Prov.), d. 1941 at New York. Long-time resident of Berlin; in 1933, fled from the Nazis to Russia, later to the USA. Won the world title in 1894 by defeating Steinitz and defended it seven times before relinquishing it to Capablanca in 1921. His greatest tournament victories: St Petersburg 1895, Nuremberg 1896, London 1898, Paris 1900, St Petersburg 1909 (first equal with Rubinstein), St Petersburg 1914, Berlin 1918, Mährisch-Ostrau 1923, New York 1924 (as former world champion over Capablanca and Alekhin). He won a last magnificent victory in the heavily attended tournament at Moscow in 1935, when he was sixty-six years old, obtaining a very good third place below Botvinnik and Flohr.

Klaus Lindorfer
Großes Schach-Lexikon
Munich 1981

Chess players may be interested to know the actual moves played in the crucial tenth and final game of the World Championship match held in Berlin in 1910 between Emanuel Lasker (white) and Karl Schlechter (black):

1. d4	d5	25. Qb3+	Rf7	49. Kb3	Bg7		
2. c4	c6	26. Qxb7	Raf8!	50. Ne6	Qb2+		
3. Nf3	Nf6	27. Qb3	Kh8	51. Ka4	Kf7		
4. e3	g6	28. f4	g5!	52. Nxg7	Qxg7		
5. Nc3	Bg7	29. Qd3	gxf4	53. Qb3	Ke8		
6. Bd3	o – o	30.exf4	Qh4+	54. Qb8+	Kf7		
7. Qc2	Na6	31. Ke2	Qh2+	55. Qxa7	Qg4+		
8. a3	dxc4	32. Rf2	Qh5+	56. Qd4	Qd7+		
9. Bxc4	b5	33. Rf3	Nc7!	57. Kb3	Qb7+		
10. Bd3	b4	34. Rxc6?!	Nb5∓	58. Ka2	Qc6		
11. Na4	bxa3	35.Rc4!	Rxf4?	59. Qd3	Ke6		
12. bxa3	Bb7	36. Bxf4	Rxf4	60. Rg5	Kd7		
13. Rb1	Qc7	37. Rc8+	Bf8	61. Re5	Qg2+		
14. Ne5?!	Nh5	38. Kf2!	Qh2+	62. Re2	Qg4		
15. g4?	Bxe5	39. Ke1	Qh1+?+–	63. Rd2	Qa4		
16. gxh5	Bg7	40. Rf1	Qh4+	64. Qf5+	Kc7?		
17. hxg6	hxg6	41. Kd2	Rxf1	65. Qc2+	Qxc2+		
18. Qc4	Bc8!	42. Qxf1	Qxd4+	66. Rxc2+	Kb7		
19. Rg1?!	Qa5+	43. Qd3	Qf2+	67. Re2	Nc8		
20. Bd2	Qd5	44. Kd1	Nd6	68. Kb3	Kc6		
21. Rc1	Bb7	45. Rc5	Bh6	69. Rc2+	Kb7		
22. Qc2	Qh5	46. Rd5	Kg8?	70. Kb4	Na7		
23. Bxg6?	Qxh2!	47. Nc5	Qg1+	71. Kc5			
24. Rf1	fxg6	48. Kc2	Qf2+